ST. MAWR

LECTOR HOUSE PUBLIC DOMAIN WORKS

ST. MAWR

DAVID HERBERT LAWRENCE

ISBN: 978-93-5344-079-4

First Published: -

© LECTOR HOUSE LLP

LECTOR HOUSE LLP
E-MAIL: lectorpublishing@gmail.com

ST. MAWR

BY

D. H. LAWRENCE

ST. MAWR

Lou Witt had had her own way so long, that by the age of twenty-five she didn't know where she was. Having one's own way landed one completely at sea.

To be sure for a while she had failed in her grand love affair with Rico. And then she had had something really to despair about. But even that had worked out as she wanted. Rico had come back to her, and was dutifully married to her. And now, when she was twenty-five and he was three months older, they were a charming married couple. He flirted with other women still, to be sure. He wouldn't be the 'handsome Rico if he didn't. But she had 'got' him. Oh yes! You had only to see the uneasy backward glance at her, from his big blue eyes: just like a horse that is edging away from its master: to know how completely he was mastered.

She, with her odd little museau, not exactly pretty, but very attractive; and her quaint air of playing at being well bred, in a sort of charade game; and her queer familiarity with foreign cities and foreign languages; and the lurking sense of being an outsider everywhere, like a sort of gipsy, who is at home anywhere and nowhere: all this made up her charm and her failure. She didn't quite belong.

Of course she was American: Louisiana family, moved down to Texas. And she was moderately rich, with no close relation except her mother. But she had been sent to school in France when she was twelve, and since she had finished school, she had drifted from Paris to Palermo, Biarritz to Vienna and back via Munich to London, then down again to Rome. Only fleeting trips to her America.

So what sort of American was she, after all?

And what sort of European was she either? She didn't 'belong' anywhere. Perhaps most of all in Rome, among the artists and the Embassy people.

It was in Rome she had met Rico. He was an Australian, son of a government official in Melbourne, who had been made a baronet. So one day Rico would be Sir Henry, as he was the only son. Meanwhile he floated round Europe on a very small allowance--his father wasn't rich in capital--and was being an artist.

They met in Rome when they were twenty-two, and had a love affair in Capri. Rico was handsome, elegant, but mostly he had spots of paint on his trousers and he ruined a neck-tie pulling it off. He behaved in a most floridly elegant fashion, fascinating to the Italians. But at the same time he was canny and shrewd and sensible as any young poser could be and, on principle, good-hearted, anxious. He was anxious for his future, and anxious for his place in the world, he was poor, and suddenly wasteful in spite of all his tension of economy, and suddenly spiteful in spite of all his ingratiating efforts, and suddenly ungrateful in spite of all his burden of gratitude, and suddenly rude in spite of all his good manners, and suddenly detestable in spite of all his suave, courtier-like amiability.

He was fascinated by Lou's quaint aplomb, her experiences, her 'knowledge', her *gamine* knowingness, her aloneness, her pretty clothes that were sometimes an utter failure, and her southern 'drawl' that was sometimes so irritating. That singsong which was so American. Yet she used no Americanisms at all, except when she lapsed into her odd spasms of acid irony, when she was very American indeed!

And she was fascinated by Rico. They played to each other like two butterflies at one flower. They pretended to be very poor in Rome--he was poor: and very rich in Naples. Everybody stared their eyes out at them. And they had that love affair in Capri.

But they reacted badly on each other's nerves. She became ill. Her mother appeared. He couldn't stand Mrs. Witt, and Mrs. Witt couldn't stand him. There was a terrible fortnight. Then Lou was popped into a convent nursing-home in Umbria, and Rico dashed off to Paris. Nothing would stop him. He must go back to Australia.

He went to Melbourne, and while there his father died, leaving him a baronet's title and an income still very moderate. Lou visited America once more, as the strangest of strange lands to her. She came away disheartened, panting for Europe, and, of course, doomed to meet Rico again.

They couldn't get away from one another, even though in the course of their rather restrained correspondence he informed her that he was 'probably' marrying a very dear girl, friend of his childhood, only daughter of one of the oldest families in Victoria. Not saying much.

He didn't commit the probability, but reappeared in Paris, wanting to paint his head off, terribly inspired by Cézanne and by old Renoir. He dined at the Rotonde with Lou and Mrs. Witt, who, with her queer democratic New Orleans sort of conceit, looked round the drinking-hall with savage contempt, and at Rico as part of the show. "Certainly," she said, "when these people here have got any money, they fall in love on a full stomach. And when they've got no money, they fall in love with a full pocket. I never was in a more disgusting place. They take their love like some people take after-dinner pills."

She would watch with her arching, full, strong grey eyes, sitting there erect and silent in her well-bought American clothes. And then she would deliver some such charge of grape-shot. Rico always writhed.

Mrs. Witt hated Paris: "this sordid, unlucky city," she called it. "Something unlucky is bound to happen to me in this sinister, unclean town," she said. "I feel contagion in the air of this place. For heaven's sake, Louise, let us go to Morocco or somewhere."

"No, mother dear, I can't now. Rico has proposed to me, and I have accepted him. Let us think about a wedding, shall we?"

"There!" said Mrs. Witt. "I said it was an unlucky city!"

And the peculiar look of extreme New Orleans annoyance came round her sharp nose. But Lou and Rico were both twenty-four years old, and beyond management. And, anyhow, Lou would be Lady Carrington. But Mrs. Witt was exasperated beyond exasperation. She would almost rather have preferred Lou to elope with one of the great, evil porters at Les Halles. Mrs. Witt was at the age when the malevolent male in man, the old Adam, begins to loom above all the social tailoring. And yet--and yet--it was better to have Lady Carrington for a daughter, seeing Lou was that sort.

There was a marriage, after which Mrs. Witt departed to America, Lou and Rico leased a little old house in Westminster, and began to settle into a certain layer of English society. Rico was becoming an almost fashionable portrait-painter. At least, he was almost fashionable, whether his portraits were or not. And Lou, too, was almost fashionable: almost a hit. There was some flaw somewhere. In spite of their appearances, both Rico and she would never quite go down in any society. They were the drifting artist sort. Yet neither of them was content to be of the drifting artist sort. They wanted to fit in, to make good.

Hence the little house in Westminster, the portraits, the dinners, the friends, and the visits. Mrs. Witt came and sardonically established herself in a suite in a quiet but good-class hotel not far off. Being on the spot. And her terrible grey eyes with the touch of a leer looked on at the hollow mockery of things. As if she knew of anything better!

Lou and Rico had a curious exhausting effect on one another: neither knew why. They were fond of one another. Some inscrutable bond held them together. But it was a strange vibration of the nerves, rather than of the blood. A nervous attachment, rather than a sexual love. A curious tension of will, rather than a spontaneous passion. Each was curiously under the domination of the other. They were a pair--they had to be together. Yet quite soon they shrank from one another. This attachment of the will and the nerves was destructive. As soon as one felt strong, the other felt ill. As soon as the ill one recovered strength, down went the one who had been well.

And soon, tacitly, the marriage became more like a friendship, platonic. It was a marriage, but without sex. Sex was shattering and exhausting, they shrank from it, and became like brother and sister. But still they were husband and wife. And the lack of physical relation was a secret source of uneasiness and chagrin to both of them. They would neither of them accept it. Rico looked with contemplative, anxious eyes at other women.

Mrs. Witt kept track of everything, watching, as it were, from outside the fence, like a potent well-dressed demon, full of uncanny energy and a shattering sort of sense. She said little: but her small, occasionally biting remarks revealed her attitude of contempt for the *ménage*.

Rico entertained clever and well-known people. Mrs. Witt would appear, in her New York gowns and few good jewels. She was handsome, with her vigorous grey hair. But her heavy-lidded grey eyes were the despair of any hostess. They looked too many shattering things. And it was but too obvious that these clever, well-known English people got on her nerves terribly, with their finickiness and their fine-drawn discriminations. She wanted to put her foot through all these fine-drawn distinctions. She thought continually of the house of her girlhood, the plantation, the negroes, the planters: the sardonic grimness that underlay all the big, shiftless life. And she wanted to cleave with some of this grimness of the big, dangerous America, into the safe, finicky drawing-rooms of London. So naturally she was not popular.

But being a woman of energy, she had to do *something*. During the latter part of the war she had worked in the American Red Cross in France, nursing. She loved men--real men. But, on close contact, it was difficult to define what she meant by 'real' men. She never met any.

Out of the *débacle* of the war she had emerged with an odd piece of débris, in the shape of Geronimo Trujillo. He was an American, son of a Mexican father and a Navajo Indian mother, from Arizona. When you knew him well, you recognised the real half-breed, though at a glance he might pass as a sunburnt citizen of any nation, particularly of France. He looked like a certain sort of Frenchman, with his curiously-set dark eyes, his straight black hair, his thin black moustache, his rather long cheeks, and his almost slouching, diffident, sardonic bearing. Only when you knew him, and looked right into his eyes, you saw that unforgettable glint of the Indian.

He had been badly shell-shocked, and was for a time a wreck. Mrs. Witt, having nursed him into convalescence, asked him where he was going next. He didn't know. His father and mother were dead, and he had nothing to take him back to Phoenix, Arizona. Having had an education in one of the Indian high schools, the unhappy fellow had now no place in life at all. Another of the many misfits.

There was something of the Paris *Apache* in his appearance but he was all the time withheld, and nervously shut inside himself. Mrs. Witt was intrigued by him.

"Very well, Phoenix," she said, refusing to adopt his Spanish name, "I'll see what I can do."

What she did was to get him a place on a sort of manor farm, with some acquaintances of hers. He was very good with horses, and had a curious success with turkeys and geese and fowls.

Some time after Lou's marriage, Mrs. Witt reappeared in London, from the country, with Phoenix in tow, and a couple of horses. She had decided that she would ride in the Park in the morning, and see the world that way. Phoenix was to be her groom.

So, to the great misgiving of Rico, behold Mrs. Witt in splendidly tailored habit and perfect boots, a smart black hat on her smart grey hair, riding a grey gelding as smart as she was, and looking down her conceited, inquisitive, scornful, aristocratic-democratic Louisiana nose at the people in Piccadilly, as she crossed to the Row, followed by the taciturn shadow of Phoenix, who sat on a chestnut with three white feet as if he had grown there.

Mrs. Witt, like many other people, always expected to find the real *beau monde* and the real *grand monde* somewhere or other. She didn't quite give in to what she saw in the Bois de Boulogne, or in Monte Carlo, or on the Pincio: all a bit shoddy, and not very *beau* and not at all *grand*. There she was, with her grey eagle eye, her splendid complexion and her weapon-like health of a woman of fifty, dropping her eyelids a little, very slightly nervous, but completely prepared to despise the *monde* she was entering in Rotten Row.

In she sailed, and up and down that regatta-canal of horsemen and horsewomen under the trees of the Park. And yes, there were lovely girls with fair hair down their backs, on happy ponies. And awfully well-groomed papas, arid tight mamas who looked as if they were going to pour tea between the ears of their horses, and converse with banal skill, one eye on the teapot, one on the visitor with whom she was talking, and all the rest of her hostess's argus eyes upon everybody in sight. That alert argus capability of the English matron was startling and a bit horrifying. Mrs. Witt would at once think of the old negro mammies, away in Louisiana. And her eyes became dagger-like as she watched the clipped, shorn, mincing young Englishmen. She refused to look at the prosperous Jews.

It was still the days before motor-cars were allowed in the Park, but Rico and Lou, sliding round Hyde Park Corner and up Park Lane in their car, would watch the steely horsewoman and the saturnine groom with a sort of dismay. Mrs. Witt seemed to be pointing a pistol at the bosom of every other horseman or horsewoman and announcing: *"Your virility or your life! Your femininity or your life!"* She didn't know herself what she really wanted them to be: but it was something as democratic as Abraham Lincoln and as aristocratic as a Russian czar, as highbrow as Arthur Balfour, and as taciturn and unideal as Phoenix. Everything at once.

There was nothing for it: Lou had to buy herself a horse and ride at her mother's side, for very decency's sake. Mrs. Witt was so like a smooth, levelled, gun-metal pistol, Lou had to be a sort of sheath. And she really looked pretty, with her clusters of dark, curly, New Orleans hair, like grapes, and her quaint brown eyes that didn't quite match, and that looked a bit sleepy and vague, and at the same time quick as a squirrel's. She was slight and elegant, and a tiny bit rakish, and somebody suggested she might be on the movies.

Nevertheless, they were in the society columns next morning--*two new and striking figures in the Row this morning were Lady Henry Carrington and her mother, Mrs. Witt, etc.* And Mrs. Witt liked it, let her say what she might. So did Lou. Lou liked it immensely. She simply luxuriated in the sun of publicity.

"Rico dear, you must get a horse."

The tone was soft and southern and drawling, but the overtone had a decisive finality. In vain Rico squirmed--he had a way of writhing and squirming which perhaps he had caught at Oxford. In vain he protested that he couldn't ride, and that he didn't care for riding. He got quite angry, and his handsome arched nose tilted and his upper lip lifted from his teeth, like a dog that is going to bite. Yet daren't quite bite.

And that was Rico. He daren't quite bite. Not that he was really afraid of the others. He was afraid of himself, once he let himself go. He might rip up in an eruption of life-long anger all this pretty-pretty picture of a charming young wife and a delightful little home and a fascinating success as a painter of fashionable, and at the same time 'great' portraits: with colour, wonderful colour, and at the same time, form, marvellous form. He had composed this little tableau vivant with great effort. He didn't want to erupt like some suddenly wicked horse--Rico was really more like a horse than a dog, a horse that might go nasty any moment. For the time, he was good, very good, dangerously good.

"Why, Rico dear, I thought you used to ride so much, in Australia, when you were young? Didn't you tell me all about it, hm?"--and as she ended on that slow, singing *hm?*, which acted on him like an irritant and a drug, he knew he was beaten.

Lou kept the sorrel mare in a mews just behind the house in Westminster, and she was always slipping round to the stables. She had a funny little nostalgia for the place: something that really surprised her. She had never had the faintest notion that she cared for horses and stables and grooms. But she did. She was fascinated. Perhaps it was her childhood's Texas associations come back. Whatever it was, her life with Rico in the elegant little house, and all her social engagements seemed like a dream, the substantial reality of which was those mews in Westminster, her sorrel mare, the owner of the mews, Mr. Saintsbury, and the grooms he employed. Mr. Saintsbury was a horsey, elderly man like an old maid, and he loved the sound of titles.

"Lady Carrington!--well I never! You've come to us for a bit of company again, I see. I don't know whatever we shall do if you go away, we shall be that lonely!" and he flashed his old-maid's smile at her. "No matter how grey the morning, your ladyship would make a beam of sunshine. Poppy is all right, I think..."

Poppy was the sorrel mare with the no white feet and the startled eye, and she was all right. And Mr. Saintsbury was smiling with his old-maid's mouth, and showing all his teeth.

"Come across with me, Lady Carrington, and look at a new horse just up from the country. I think he's worth a look, and I believe you have a moment to spare, your Ladyship."

Her Ladyship had too many moments to spare. She followed the sprightly, elderly, clean-shaven man across the yard to a loose-box, and waited while he opened the door.

In the inner dark she saw a handsome bay horse with his clean ears pricked like daggers from his naked head as he swung handsomely round to stare at the open doorway. He had big, black, brilliant eyes, with a sharp questioning glint, and that air of tense, alert quietness which betrays an animal that can be dangerous.

"Is he quiet?" Lou asked.

"Why--yes--my Lady! He's quiet, with those that know how to handle him. *Cup! my boy! Cup, my beauty! Cup then! St. Mawr!*"

Loquacious even with the animals, he went softly forward and laid his hand on the horse's shoulder, soft and quiet as a fly settling. Lou saw the brilliant skin of the horse crinkle a little in apprehensive anticipation, like the shadow of the descending hand on a bright red-gold liquid. But then the animal relaxed again.

"Quiet with those that know how to handle him, and a bit of a ruffian with those that don't. Isn't that the ticket, eh, St. Mawr?"

"What is his name?" Lou asked.

The man repeated it, with a slight Welsh twist--"He's from the Welsh borders, belonging to a Welsh gentleman, Mr. Griffith Edwards. But they're wanting to sell him."

"How old is he?" asked Lou.

"About seven years--seven years and five months," said Mr. Saintsbury, dropping his voice as if it were a secret. "Could one ride him in the Park?"

"Well--yes! I should say a gentleman who knew how to handle him could ride him very well and make a very handsome figure in the Park."

Lou at once decided that this handsome figure should be Rico's. For she was already half in love with St. Mawr. He was of such a lovely red-gold colour, and a dark, invisible fire seemed to come out of him. But in his big black eyes there was a lurking afterthought. Something told her that the horse was not quite happy: that somewhere deep in his animal consciousness lived a dangerous, half-revealed resentment, a diffused sense of hostility. She realised that he was sensitive, in spite of his flaming, healthy strength, and nervous with a touchy uneasiness that might make him vindictive.

"Has he got any tricks?" she asked.

"Not that I know of, my Lady: not tricks exactly. But he's one of these temperamental creatures, as they say. Though I say, every horse is temperamental, when you come down to it. But this one, it is as if he was a trifle raw somewhere. Touch this raw spot, and there's no answering for him."

"Where is he raw?" asked Lou, somewhat mystified. She thought he might really have some physical sore.

"Why, that's hard to say, my Lady. If he was a human being, you'd say something had gone wrong in his life. But with a horse it's not that, exactly. A high-bred animal like St. Mawr needs understanding, and I don't know as anybody has quite got the hang of him. I confess I haven't myself. But I do realise that he is a special animal and needs a special sort of touch, and I'm willing he should have it, did I but know exactly what it is."

She looked at the glowing bay horse that stood there with his ears back, his face averted, but attending as if he were some lightning-conductor. He was a stallion. When she realised this, she became more afraid of him.

"Why does Mr. Griffith Edwards want to sell him?" she asked.

"Well--my Lady--they raised him for stud purposes--but he didn't answer. There are horses like that: don't seem to fancy the mares for some reason. Well, anyway, they couldn't keep him for the stud. And as you see, he's a powerful, beautiful hackney, clean as a whistle, and eaten up with his own power. But there's no putting him between the shafts. He won't stand it. He's a fine saddle-horse, beautiful action, and lovely to ride. But he's got to be handled, and there you are."

Lou felt there was something behind the man's reticence.

"Has he ever made a break?" she asked, apprehensive.

"Made a break?" replied the man. "Well, if I must admit it, he's had two accidents. Mr. Griffith Edwards's son rode him a bit wild, away there in the Forest of Dean, and the young fellow had his skull smashed in against a low oak bough. Last autumn, that was. And some time back, he crushed a groom against the side of the stall--injured him fatally. But they were both accidents, my Lady. Things will happen."

The man spoke in a melancholy, fatalistic way. The horse, with his ears laid back, seemed to be listening tensely, his face averted. He looked like something finely bred and passionate that has been judged and condemned.

"May I say *how do you do?*" she said to the horse, drawing a little nearer in her white, summery dress and lifting her hand that glittered with emeralds and diamonds.

He drifted away from her, as if some wind blew him. Then he ducked his head and looked sideway at her from his black, full eye.

"I think I'm all right," she said, edging nearer, while he watched her.

She laid her hand on his side and gently stroked him. Then she stroked his shoulder, and then the hard, tense arch of his neck. And she was startled to feel the vivid heat of his life come through to her, through the lacquer of red-gold gloss. So slippery with vivid, hot life!

She paused, as if thinking, while her hand rested on the horse's sun-arched neck. Dimly, in her weary young woman's soul, an ancient understanding seemed to flood in. She wanted to buy St. Mawr.

"I think," she said to Saintsbury, "if I can, I will buy him." The man looked at her long and shrewdly.

"Well, my Lady," he said at last, "there shall be nothing kept from you. But what would your Ladyship do with him, if I may make so bold?"

"I don't know," she replied vaguely. "I might take him to America."

The man paused once more, then said:

"They say it's been the making of some horses, to take them over the water, to Australia or such places. It might repay you--you never know."

She wanted to buy St. Mawr. She wanted him to belong to her. For some reason the sight of him, his power, his alive, alert intensity, his unyieldingness, made her want to cry.

She never did cry: except sometimes with vexation, or to get her own way. As far as weeping went, her heart felt as dry as a Christmas walnut. What was the good of tears, anyhow? You had to keep on holding on in this life, never give way, and never give in. Tears only left one weakened and ragged.

But now, as if that mysterious fire of the horse's body had split some rock in her, she went home and hid herself in her room, and just cried. The wild, brilliant, alert head of St. Mawr seemed to look at her out of another world. It was as if she had had a vision, as if the walls of her Awn world had suddenly melted away, leaving her in a great darkness, in the midst of which the large, brilliant eyes of that horse looked at her with demonish question, while his naked ears stood up like daggers from the naked lines of his inhuman head, and his great body glowed red with power.

What was it? Almost like a god looking at her terribly out of the everlasting dark, she had felt the eyes of that horse; great, glowing, fearsome eyes, arched with a question and containing a white blade of light like a threat. What was his non-human question, and his uncanny threat? She didn't know. He was some splendid demon, and she must worship him.

She hid herself away from Rico. She could not bear the triviality and superficiality of her human relationships. Looming like some god out of the darkness was the head of that horse, with the wide, terrible, questioning eyes. And she felt that it forbade her to be her ordinary, commonplace self. It forbade her to be just Rico's wife, young Lady Carrington, and all that.

It haunted her, the horse. It had looked at her as she had never been looked at before: terrible, gleaming, questioning eyes arching out of darkness, and backed by all the fire of that great ruddy body. What did it mean, and what ban did it put upon her? She felt it put a ban on her heart: wielded some uncanny authority over her, that she dared not, could not understand.

No matter where she was, what she was doing, at the back of her consciousness loomed a great, over-aweing figure out of a dark background: St. Mawr, looking at her without really seeing her, yet gleaming a question at her, from his wide, terrible eyes, and gleaming a sort of menace, doom. Master of doom, he seemed to be!

"You are thinking about something, Lou dear!" Rico said to her that evening.

He was so quick and sensitive to detect her moods--so exciting in this respect. And his big, slightly prominent blue eyes, with the whites a little bloodshot, glanced at her quickly, with searching and anxiety, and a touch of fear, as if his conscience were always uneasy. He, too, was rather like a horse--but forever quivering with a sort of cold, dangerous mistrust, which he covered with anxious love.

At the middle of his eyes was a central powerlessness that left him anxious. It used to touch her to pity, that central look of powerlessness in him. But now, since she had seen the full, dark, passionate blaze of power and of different life in the eyes of the thwarted horse, the anxious powerlessness of the man drove her mad. Rico was so handsome, and he was so self-controlled, he had a gallant sort of kindness and a real worldly shrewdness. One had to admire him: at least she had to.

But after all, and after all, it was a bluff, an attitude. He kept it all working in himself deliberately. It was an attitude.

She read psychologists who said that everything was an attitude. Even the best of everything. But now she realised that, with men and women, everything is an attitude only when something else is lacking. Something is lacking and they are thrown back on their own devices. That black fiery flow in the eyes of the horse was not 'attitude'. It was something much more terrifying, and real, the only thing that was real. Gushing from the darkness in menace and question, and blazing out in the splendid body of the horse.

"Was I thinking about something?" she replied in her slow, amused, casual fashion. As if everything was so casual and easy to her. And so it was, from the hard, polished side of herself. But that wasn't the whole story.

"I think you were, Loulina. May we offer the penny?"

"Don't trouble," she said. "I was thinking, if I was thinking of anything, about a bay horse called St. Mawr."--Her secret *almost* crept into her eyes.

"The name is awfully attractive," he said with a laugh. "Not so attractive as the creature himself. I'm going to buy him."

"Not really!" he said. "But why?"

"He is so attractive. I'm going to buy him for you."

"For *me? Darling?* How you do take me for granted. He may not be in the least attractive to me. As you know, I have hardly any feeling for horses at all.--Besides, how much does he cost?"

"That I don't know, Rico dear. But I'm sure you'll love him, for my sake."--She felt, now, she was merely playing for her own ends.

"Lou dearest, *don't* spend a fortune on a horse for me, which I *don't* want. Honestly, I prefer a car."

"Won't you ride with me in the Park, Rico?"

"Honestly, dear Lou, I don't want to."

"Why not, dear boy? You look so beautiful. I wish you would.--And, anyhow, come with me to look at St. Mawr."

Rico was divided. He had a certain uneasy feeling about horses. At the same time, he would like to cut a handsome figure in the Park.

They went across to the mews. A little Welsh groom was watering the brilliant horse.

"Yes, dear, he certainly is beautiful: such a marvellous colour! Almost orange! But rather large, I should say, to ride in the Park."

"No, for you he's perfect. You are so tall."

"He'd be marvellous in a Composition. That colour!" And all Rico could do was to gaze with the artist's eye at the horse, with a glance at the groom.

"Don't you think the man is rather fascinating too?" he said, nursing his chin artistically and penetratingly. The groom, Lewis, was a little, quick, rather bow-legged, loosely-built fellow of indeterminate age, with a mop of black hair and a little black beard. He was grooming the brilliant St. Mawr out in the open. The horse was really glorious: like a marigold, with a pure golden sheen, a shimmer of green-gold lacquer upon a burning red-orange. There on the shoulder you saw the yellow lacquer glisten. Lewis, a little scrub of a fellow, worked absorbedly, un-heedingly at the horse, with an absorption that was almost ritualistic. He seemed the attendant shadow of the ruddy animal.

"He goes with the horse," said Lou. "If we buy St. Mawr we get the man thrown in."

"They'd be *so* amusing to paint; such an extraordinary contrast! But darling, I *hope* you won't insist on buying the horse. It's so frightfully expensive."

"Mother will help me.--You'd look so well on him, Rico."

"If ever I dared take the liberty of getting on his back----!"

"Why not?" She went quickly across the cobbled yard. "Good morning, Lewis. How is St. Mawr?"

Lewis straightened himself and looked at her from under the falling mop of his black hair.

"All right," he said.

He peered straight at her from under his overhanging black hair. He had pale grey eyes, that looked phosphorescent, and suggested the eyes of a wild cat peering intent from under the darkness of some bush where it lies unseen. Lou, with her brown, unmatched, oddly perplexed eyes, felt herself found out.--"He's a common little fellow," she thought to herself. "But he knows a woman and a horse at sight."--Aloud she said, in her Southern drawl:

"How do you think he'd be with Sir Henry?"

Lewis turned his remote, coldly watchful eyes on the young baronet. Rico was tall and handsome and balanced on his hips. His face was long and well-defined, and with the hair taken straight back from the brow. It seemed as well-made as his clothing, and as perpetually presentable. You could not imagine his face dirty, or scrubby and unshaven, or bearded, or even moustached. It was perfectly prepared for social purposes. If his head had been cut off, like John the Baptist's, it would have been a thing complete in itself, would not have missed the body in the least. The body was perfectly tailored. The head was one of the famous 'talking heads' of modern youth, with eyebrows a trifle Mephistophelian, large blue eyes a trifle hold, and curved mouth thrilling to death to kiss.

Lewis, the groom, staring from between his bush of hair and his beard, watched like an animal from the underbrush. And Rico was still sufficiently a colonial to be uneasily aware of the underbrush, uneasy under the watchfulness of the pale grey eyes, and uneasy in that man-to-man exposure which is characteristic of the democratic colonies and of America. He knew he must ultimately be judged on his merits as a man, alone without a background: an ungarnished colonial.

This lack of background, this defenceless man-to-man business which left him at the mercy of every servant, was bad for his nerves. For he was also an artist. He bore up against it in a kind of desperation, and was easily moved to rancorous resentment. At the same time he was free of the Englishman's water-tight *suffisance*. He really was aware that he would have to hold his own all alone, thrown alone on his own defences in the universe. The extreme democracy of the Colonies had taught him this.

And this, the little aboriginal Lewis recognised in him. He recognised also Rico's curious hollow misgiving, fear of some deficiency in himself, beneath all his handsome, young-hero appearance.

"He'd be all right with anybody as would meet him halfway," said Lewis, in the quick Welsh manner of speech, impersonal.

"You hear, Rico!" said Lou in her sing-song, turning to her husband.

"Perfectly, darling!"

"Would you be willing to meet St. Mawr half-way, hm?"

"All the way, darling! Mahomet would go all the way to that mountain. Who would dare do otherwise?"

He spoke with a laughing, yet piqued sarcasm.

"Why, I think St. Mawr would understand perfectly," she said in the soft voice of a woman haunted by love. And she went and laid her hand on the slippery, life-smooth shoulder of the horse. He, with his strange equine head lowered, its exquisite fine lines reaching a little snake-like forward, and his ears a little back, was watching her sideways from the corner of his eye. He was in a state of absolute mistrust, like a cat crouching to spring.

"St. Mawr!" she said. "St. Mawr! What is the matter? Surely you and I are all right!"

And she spoke softly, dreamily stroked the animal's neck. She could feel a response gradually coming from him. But he would not lift up his head. And when Rico suddenly moved nearer, he sprang with a sudden jerk backwards, as if lightning exploded in his four hoofs.

The groom spoke a few low words in Welsh. Lou, frightened, stood with lifted hands arrested. She had been going to stroke him.

"Why did he do that?" she said.

"They gave him a beating once or twice," said the groom in a neutral voice, "and he doesn't forget."

She could hear a neutral sort of judgment in Lewis's voice. And she thought of the 'raw spot'.

Not any raw spot at all. A battle between two worlds. She realised that St. Mawr drew his hot breaths in another world from Rico's, from our world. Perhaps the old Greek horses had lived in St. Mawr's world. And the old Greek heroes, even Hippolytus, had known it.

With their strangely naked equine heads, and something of a snake in their way of looking round, and lifting their sensitive, dangerous muzzles, they moved in a prehistoric twilight where all things loomed phantasmagoric, all on one plane, sudden presences suddenly jutting out of the matrix. It was another world, an older, heavily potent world. And in this world the horse was swift and fierce and supreme, undominated and unsurpassed.--"Meet him half-way," Lewis said. But half-way across from our human world to that terrific equine twilight was not a small step. It was a step, she knew, that Rico could never take. She knew it. But she was prepared to sacrifice Rico.

St. Mawr was bought, and Lewis was hired along with him. At first, Lewis rode him behind Lou, in the Row, to get him going. He behaved perfectly.

Phoenix, the half Indian, was very jealous when he saw the black-bearded Welsh groom on St. Mawr.

"What horse you got there?" he asked, looking at the other man with the curious unseeing stare in his hard, Navajo eyes, in which the Indian glint moved like a spark upon a dark chaos. In Phoenix's high-boned face there was all the race misery of the dispossessed Indian, with an added blankness left by shell-shock. But at the same time, there was that unyielding, save to death, which is characteristic of his tribe; his mother's tribe. Difficult to say what subtle thread bound him to the Navajo, and made his destiny a Red Man's destiny still.

They were a curious pair of grooms, following the correct, and yet extraordinary, pair of American mistresses. Mrs. Witt and Phoenix both rode with long stirrups and straight leg, sitting close to the saddle, without posting. Phoenix looked as if he and the horse were all one piece, he never seemed to rise in the saddle at all, neither trotting nor galloping, but sat like a man riding bareback. And all the time he stared around at the riders in the Row, at the people grouped outside the rail, chatting, at the children walking with their nurses, as if he were looking at a mirage, in whose actuality he never believed for a moment. London was all a sort of dark mirage to him. His wide, nervous-looking brown eyes with a smallish brown pupil, that showed the white all round, seemed to be focused on the far distance, as if he could not see things too near. He was watching the pale deserts of Arizona shimmer with moving light, the long mirage of a shallow lake ripple, the great pallid concave of earth and sky expanding with interchanged light. And a horse-shape loom large and portentous in the mirage, like some prehistoric beast.

That was real to him: the phantasm of Arizona. But this London was something his eye passed over as a false mirage. He looked too smart in his well-tailored groom's clothes, so smart, he might have been one of the satirised new rich. Perhaps it was a sort of half-breed physical assertion that came through his clothing, the savage's physical assertion of himself. Anyhow, he looked 'common', rather horsey and loud.

Except his face. In the golden suavity of his high-boned Indian face, that was hairless, with hardly any eyebrows, there was a blank, lost look that was almost touching. The same startled blank look was in his eyes. But in the smallish dark pupils the dagger-point of light still gleamed unbroken.

He was a good groom, watchful, quick, and on the spot in an instant if anything went wrong. He had a curious quiet power over the horses, unemotional, unsympathetic, but silently potent. In the same way, watching the traffic of Piccadilly with his blank, glinting eye, he would calculate everything instinctively, as if it were an enemy, and pilot Mrs. Witt by the strength of his silent will. He threw around her the tense watchfulness of her own America, and made her feel at home.

"Phoenix," she said, turning abruptly in her saddle as they walked the horses past the sheltering policeman at Hyde Park Corner, "I can't tell you how glad I am to have something a hundred per cent American at the back of me when I go through these gates."

She looked at him from dangerous grey eyes as if she meant it indeed, in vindictive earnest. A ghost of a smile went up to his high cheek-bones, but he did not answer.

"Why, mother?" said Lou, sing-song. "It feels to me so friendly--!"

"Yes, Louise, it does. So friendly! That's why I mistrust it so entirely--"

And she set off at a canter up the Row, under the green trees, her face like the face of Medusa at fifty, a weapon in itself. She stared at everything and everybody, with that stare of cold dynamite waiting to explode them all. Lou posted trotting at her side, graceful and elegant, and faintly amused. Behind came Phoenix, like a shadow, with his yellowish, high-boned face still looking sick. And at his side, on the big brilliant bay horse, the smallish, black-bearded Welshman.

Between Phoenix and Lewis there was a latent, but unspoken and wary sympathy. Phoenix was terribly impressed by St. Mawr, he could not leave off staring at him. And Lewis rode the brilliant, handsome-moving stallion so very quietly, like an insinuation.

Of the two men, Lewis looked the darker, with his black beard coming up to his thick black eyebrows. He was swarthy, with a rather short nose, and the uncanny pale-grey eyes that watched everything and cared about nothing. He cared about nothing in the world, except, at the present, St. Mawr. People did not matter to him. He rode his horse and watched the world from the vantage ground of St. Mawr, with a final indifference.

"You have been with that horse long?" asked Phoenix. "Since he was born."

Phoenix watched the action of St. Mawr as they went. The bay moved proud and springy, but with perfect good sense, among the stream of riders. It was a beautiful June morning, the leaves overhead were thick and green; there came the first whiff of lime tree scent. To Phoenix, however, the city was a sort of nightmare mirage, and to Lewis, it was a sort of prison. The presence of people he felt as a prison around him.

Mrs. Witt and Lou were turning at the end of the Row, bowing to some acquaintances. The grooms pulled aside Mrs. Witt looked at Lewis with a cold eye.

"It seems an extraordinary thing to me, Louise," she said, "to see a groom with a beard."

"It isn't usual, mother," said Lou. "Do you mind?"

"Not at all. At least, I think I don't. I get very tired of modern, bare-faced young men, very! The clean, pure boy, don't you know! Doesn't it make you tired?--No, I think a groom with a beard is quite attractive."

She gazed into the crowd defiantly, perching her finely-shod toe with war-like firmness on the stirrup-iron. Then suddenly she reined in, and turned her horse towards the grooms.

"Lewis!" she said, "I want to ask you a question. Supposing, now, that Lady Carrington wanted you to shave off that beard, what should you say?"

Lewis instinctively put up his hand to the said beard. "They've wanted me to shave it off, Mam," he said. "But I've never done it."

"But why? Tell me why?"

"It's part of me, Mam."

Mrs. Witt pulled on again.

"Isn't that extraordinary, Louise?" she said. "Don't you like the way he says Mam? It sounds so impossible to me. Could any woman think of herself as Mam? Never!--Since Queen Victoria. But, do you know it hadn't occurred to me that a man's beard was really part of him. It always seemed to me that men wore their beards, like they wear their neckties, for show. I shall always remember Lewis for saying his beard was part of him. Isn't it curious, the way he rides? He seems to sink himself in the horse. When I speak to him, I'm not sure whether I'm speaking to a man or to a horse."

A few days later, Rico himself appeared on St. Mawr for the morning ride. He rode self-consciously, as he did everything, and he was just a little nervous. But his mother-in-law was benevolent. She made him ride between her and Lou, like three ships slowly sailing abreast.

And that very day, who should come driving in an open carriage through the Park but the Queen Mother! Dear old Queen Alexandra, there was a flutter everywhere. And she bowed expressly to Rico, mistaking him, no doubt, for somebody else.

"Do you know," said Rico as they sat at lunch, he and Lou and Mrs. Witt, in Mrs. Witt's sitting-room in the dark, quiet hotel in Mayfair, "I really like riding St. Mawr so much. He really is a noble animal.--If ever I am made a lord--which heaven forbid!--I shall be Lord St. Mawr."

"You mean," said Mrs. Witt, "his real lordship would be the horse?"

"Very possible, I admit," said Rico, with a curl of his long upper lip.

"Don't you think, mother," said Lou, "there is something quite noble about St. Mawr? He strikes me as the first noble thing I have ever seen."

"Certainly I've not seen any *man* that could compare with him. Because these English noblemen--well! I'd rather look at a negro Pullman-boy, if I was looking for what *I* call nobility."

Poor Rico was getting crosser and crosser. There was a devil in Mrs. Witt. She had a hard, bright devil inside her that she seemed to be able to let loose at will.

She let it loose the next day, when Rico and Lou joined her in the Row. She was silent but deadly with the horses, balking them in every way. She suddenly crowded over against the rail in front of St. Mawr, so that the stallion had to rear to pull himself up. Then, having a clear track, she suddenly set off at a gallop, like an explosion, and the stallion, all on edge, set off after her.

It seemed as if the whole Park, that morning, were in a state of nervous tension. Perhaps there was thunder in the air. But St. Mawr kept on dancing and pulling at the bit and wheeling sideways up against the railing, to the terror of the children and the onlookers, who squealed and jumped back suddenly, sending the nerves of the stallion into a rush like rockets. He reared and fought as Rico pulled him round.

Then he went on: dancing, pulling, springily progressing sideways, possessed with all the demons of perversity. Poor Rico's face grew longer and angrier. A fury rose in him, which he could hardly control. He hated his horse, and viciously tried to force him to a quiet, straight trot. Up went St. Mawr on his hind legs, to the terror of the Row. He got the bit in his teeth and began to fight.

But Phoenix, cleverly, was in front of him.

"You get off, Rico!" called Mrs. Witt's voice, with all the calm of her wicked exultance.

And almost before he knew what he was doing, Rico had sprung lightly to the ground, and was hanging on to the bridle of the rearing stallion.

Phoenix also lightly jumped down, and ran to St. Mawr, handing his bridle to Rico. Then began a dancing and a splashing, a rearing and a plunging. St. Mawr was being wicked. But Phoenix, the indifference of conflict in his face, sat tight and immovable, without any emotion, only the heaviness of his impersonal will settling down like a weight, all the time, on the horse. There was, perhaps, a curious barbaric exultance in bare, dark will devoid of emotion or personal feeling.

So they had a little display in the Row for almost five minutes, the brilliant horse rearing and fighting. Rico, with a stiff, long face, scrambled on to Phoenix's horse and withdrew to a safe distance. Policemen came, and an officious mounted policeman rode up to save the situation. But it was obvious that Phoenix, detached and apparently unconcerned, but barbarically potent in his will, would bring the horse to order.

Which he did, and rode the creature home. Rico was requested not to ride St. Mawr in the Row any more, as the stallion was dangerous to public safety. The authorities knew all about him.

Where ended the first fiasco of St. Mawr.

"We didn't get on very well with his lordship this morning," said Mrs. Witt triumphantly.

"No, he didn't like his company *at all!*" Rico snarled back. He wanted Lou to sell the horse again.

"I doubt if anyone would buy him, dear," she said. "He's a known character."

"Then make a gift of him--to your mother," said Rico with venom.

"Why to mother?" asked Lou innocently.

"She might be able to cope with him--or he with her!" The last phrase was deadly. Having delivered it, Rico departed.

Lou remained at a loss. She felt almost always a little bit dazed, as if she could not see clear nor feel clear. A curious deadness upon her, like the first touch of death. And through this cloud of numbness, or deadness, came all her muted experiences.

Why was it? She did not know. But she felt that in some way it came from a battle of wills. Her mother, Rico, herself, it was always an unspoken, unconscious battle of wills, which was gradually numbing and paralysing her. She knew Rico meant nothing but kindness by her. She knew her mother only wanted to watch over her. Yet always there was this tension of will, that was no numbing. As if at the depths of him, Rico were always angry, though he seemed so 'happy' on top. And Mrs. Witt was organically angry. So they were like a couple of bombs, timed to explode some day, but ticking on like two ordinary timepieces, in the meanwhile.

She had come definitely to realise this: that Rico's anger was wound up tight at the bottom of him, like a steel spring that kept his works going, while he himself was 'charming', like a bomb-clock with Sevres paintings or Dresden figures on the outside. But his very charm was a sort of anger, and his love was a destruction in itself. He just couldn't help it.

And she? Perhaps she was a good deal the same herself. Wound up tight inside, and enjoying herself being 'lovely'. But wound up tight on some tension that, she realised now with wonder, was really a sort of anger. This, the mainspring that drove her on the round of 'joys'.

She used really to enjoy the tension, and the élan it gave her. While she knew nothing about it. So long as she felt it really was life and happiness, this *élan*, this tension and excitement of 'enjoying oneself'.

Now suddenly she doubted the whole show. She attributed to it the curious numbness that was overcoming her, as if she couldn't feel any more.

She wanted to come unwound. She wanted to escape this battle of wills.

Only St. Mawr gave her some hint of the possibility. He was so powerful, and so dangerous. But in his dark eye, that looked, with its cloudy brown pupil, a cloud within a dark fire, like a world beyond our world, there was a dark vitality glowing, and within the fire another sort of wisdom. She felt sure of it: even when he put his ears back, and bared his teeth, and his great eyes came bolting out of his naked horse's head, and she saw demons upon demons in the chaos of his horrid eyes.

Why did he seem to her like some living background, into which she wanted to retreat? When he reared his head and neighed from his deep chest, like deep wind-bells resounding, she seemed to hear the echoes of another darker, more spacious, more dangerous, more splendid world than ours, that was beyond her. And there she wanted to go.

She kept it utterly a secret to herself. Because Rico would just have lifted his long upper lip, in his bare face, in a condescending sort of 'understanding'. And her mother would, as usual, have suspected her of side-stepping. People, all the people she knew, seemed so entirely contained within their cardboard let's-be-happy world. Their wills were fixed like machines on happiness, or fun, or the-best-ever. This ghastly cheery-o! touch, that made all her blood go numb.

Since she had really seen St. Mawr looming fiery and terrible in an outer darkness, she could not believe the world she lived in. She could not believe it was actually happening, when she was dancing in the afternoon at Claridge's, or in the evening at the Carlton, slid about with some suave young man who wasn't like a man at all to her. Or down in Sussex for the week-end with the Enderleys: the talk, the eating and drinking, the flirtation, the endless dancing: it all seemed far more bodiless and, in a strange way, wraith-like, than any fairy story. She seemed to be eating Barmecide food, that had been conjured up out of thin air, by the power of words. She seemed to be talking to handsome, young, bare-faced unrealities, not men at all: as she slid about with them, in the perpetual dance, they too seemed to have been conjured up out of air, merely for this soaring, slithering dance business. And she could not believe that, when the lights went out, they wouldn't melt back into thin air again and complete non-entity. The strange nonentity of it all! Everything just conjured up, and nothing real. '*Isn't this the best ever!*' they would beamingly assert, like wraiths of enjoyment, without any genuine substance. And she would beam back: '*Lots of fun!*'

She was thankful the season was over, and everybody was leaving London. She and Rico were due to go to Scotland, but not till August. In the meantime they would go to her mother.

Mrs. Witt had taken a cottage in Shropshire, on the Welsh border, and had moved down there with Phoenix and her horses. The open, heather-and-bilberry-covered hills were splendid for riding.

Rico consented to spend the month in Shropshire, because for near neighbours Mrs. Witt had the Manbys, at Corrabach Hall. The Manbys were rich Australians returned to the old country and set up as squires, all in full blow. Rico had known them in Victoria: they were of good family: and the girls made a great fuss of him.

So down went Lou and Rico, Lewis, Poppy and St. Mawr, to Shrewsbury, then out into the country. Mrs. Witt's 'cottage' was a tall red-brick Georgian house looking straight on to the churchyard, and the dark, looming big church.

"I never knew what a comfort it would be," said Mrs. Witt, "to have grave-stones under my drawing-room windows, and funerals for lunch."

She really did take a strange pleasure in sitting in her panelled room, that was painted grey, and watching the Dean or one of the curates officiating at the graveside, among a group of black country mourners with black-bordered hand-kerchiefs luxuriantly in use.

"Mother!" said Lou. "I think it's gruesome!"

She had a room at the back, looking over the walled garden and the stables. Nevertheless, there was the *boom! boom!* of the passing-bell, and the chiming and pealing on Sundays. The shadow of the church, indeed! A very audible shadow, making itself heard insistently.

The Dean was a big, burly, fat man with a pleasant manner. He was a gen-tleman, and a man of learning in his own line. But he let Mrs. Witt know that he looked down on her just a trifle--as a parvenu American, a Yankee--though she never was a Yankee: and at the same time he had a sincere respect for her, as a rich woman. Yes, a sincere respect for her, as a rich woman.

Lou knew that every Englishman, especially of the upper classes, has a whole-some respect for riches. But then, who hasn't?

The Dean was more *impressed* by Mrs. Witt than by little Lou. But to Lady Car-rington he was charming: she was *almost* 'one of us', you know. And he was very gracious to Rico: 'your father's splendid colonial service.'

Mrs. Witt had now a new pantomime to amuse her: the Georgian house, her own pew in church--it went with the old house: a village of thatched cottag-es--some of them with corrugated iron over the thatch: the cottage people, farm la-bourers and their families, with a few, very few, outsiders: the wicked little group of cottagers down at Mile End, famous for ill-living. The Mile-Enders were all Allisons and Jephsons, and in-bred, the Dean said: result of working through the centuries at the Quarry, and living isolated there at Mile End.

Isolated! Imagine it! A mile and a half from the railway station, ten miles from Shrewsbury. Mrs. Witt thought of Texas, and said:

"Yes, they are very isolated, away down there!"

And the Dean never for a moment suspected sarcasm.

But there she had the whole thing staged complete for her: English village life. Even miners breaking in to shatter the rather stuffy, unwholesome harmony.--All the men touched their caps to her, all the women did a bit of reverence, the chil-dren stood aside for her, if she appeared in the street.

They were all poor again: the labourers could no longer afford even a glass of beer in the evenings, since the Glorious War.

"Now I think that is terrible," said Mrs. Witt. "Not to be able to get away from those stuffy, squalid, picturesque cottages for an hour in the evening, to drink a glass of beer."

"It's a pity, I do agree with you, Mrs. Witt. But Mr. Watson has organised a men's reading-room, where the men can smoke and play dominoes, and read if they wish."

"But that," said Mrs. Witt, "is not the same as that cosy parlour in the 'Moon and Stars'."

"I quite agree," said the Dean. "It isn't"

Mrs. Witt marched to the landlord of the 'Moon and Stars' and asked for a glass of cider.

"I want," she said, in her American accent, "these poor labourers to have their glass of beer in the evenings."

"They want it themselves," said Harvey.

"Then they must have it--"

The upshot was, she decided to supply one large barrel of beer per week and the landlord was to sell it to the labourers at a penny a glass.

"My own country has gone dry," she asserted. "But not because we can't *afford* it."

By the time Lou and Rico appeared, she was deep in. She actually interfered very little: the barrel of beer was her one public act. But she *did* know everybody by sight, already, and she *did* know everybody's circumstances. And she had attended one prayer-meeting, one mothers' meeting, one sewing-bee, one 'social', one Sunday School meeting, one Band of Hope meeting, and one Sunday School treat. She ignored the poky little Wesleyan and Baptist chapels, and was true-blue Episcopalian.

"How strange these picturesque old villages are, Louise!" she said, with a duskiness around her sharp, well-bred nose. "How *easy* it all seems, all on a definite pattern. And how false! And underneath, *how corrupt!*"

She gave that queer, triumphant leer from her grey eyes, and queer demonish wrinkles seemed to twitter on her face.

Lou shrank away. She was beginning to be afraid of her mother's insatiable curiosity, that always looked for the snake under the flowers. Or rather, for the maggots.

Always this same morbid interest in other, people and their doings, their privacies, their dirty linen. Always this air of alertness for personal happenings, personalities, personalities, personalities. Always this subtle criticism and appraisal of other people, this analysis of other people's motives. If anatomy presupposes a corpse, then psychology presupposes a world of corpses. Personalities, which means personal criticism and analysis, presuppose a whole world laboratory of human psyches waiting to be vivisected. If you cut a thing up, of course it will smell. Hence, nothing raises such an infernal stink, at last, as human psychology.

Mrs. Witt was a pure psychologist, a fiendish psychologist. And Rico, in his way, was a psychologist too. But he had a formula. "Let's know the worst, dear!

But let's look on the bright side, and believe the best."

"Isn't the Dean a priceless old darling!" said Rico at breakfast.

And it had begun. Work had started in the psychic vivisection laboratory.

"Isn't he wonderful!" said Lou vaguely.

"So delightfully worldly!--*Some of us are not born to make money, dear boy. Luckily for us, we can marry it.*"--Rico made a priceless face.

"Is Mrs. Vyner so rich?" asked Lou.

"She is quite a wealthy woman--in coal," replied Mrs. Witt. "But the Dean is surely worth his weight even in gold. And he's a massive figure. I can imagine there would be great satisfaction in having him for a husband."

"Why, mother?" asked Lou.

"Oh, such a presence! One of these old Englishmen that nobody can put in their pocket. You can't imagine his wife asking him to thread her needle. Something after all so robust! So different from *young* Englishmen, who all seem to me like ladies, perfect ladies."

"*Somebody* has to keep up the tradition of the perfect lady," said Rico.

"I know it," said Mrs. Witt. "And if the women won't do it, the young gentlemen take on the burden. They bear it very well."

It was in full swing, the cut and thrust. And poor Lou, who had reached the point of stupefaction in the game, felt she did not know what to do with herself.

Rico and Mrs. Witt were deadly enemies, yet neither could keep clear of the other. It might have been they who were married to one another, their duel and their duet were so relentless.

But Rico immediately started the social round: first the Manbys: then motor twenty miles to luncheon at Lady Tewkesbury's: then young Mr. Burns came flying down in his aeroplane from Chester: then they must motor to the sea to Sir Edward Edwards's place, where there was a moonlight bathing party. Everything intensely thrilling, and so innerly wearisome, Lou felt.

But back of it all was St. Mawr, looming like a bonfire in the dark. He really was a tiresome horse to own. He worried the mares, if they were in the same paddock with him, always driving them round. And with any other horse he just fought with definite intent to kill. So he had to stay alone.

"That St. Mawr, he's a bad horse," said Phoenix.

"Maybe!" said Lewis.

"You don't like quiet horses?" said Phoenix.

"Most horses *is* quiet," said Lewis. "St. Mawr, he's different."

"Why don't he never get any foals?"

"Doesn't want to, I should think. Same as me."

"What good is a horse like that? Better shoot him, before he kill somebody."

"What good'll they get, shooting St. Mawr?" said Lewis. "If he kills somebody!" said Phoenix.

But there was no answer.

The two grooms both lived over the stables, and Lou, from her window, saw a good deal of them. They were two quiet men, yet she was very much aware of their presence, aware of Phoenix's rather high square shoulders and his fine, straight, vigorous black hair that tended to stand up assertively on his head, as he went quietly drifting about his various jobs. He was not lazy, but he did everything with a sort of diffidence, as if from a distance, and handled his horses carefully, cautiously, and cleverly, but without sympathy. He seemed to be holding something back all the time, unconsciously, as if in his very being there was some secret. But it was a secret of *will*. His quiet, reluctant movement as if he never really wanted to do anything; his long, flat-stepping stride; the permanent challenge in his high cheek-bones, the Indian glint in his eyes, and his peculiar stare, watchful and yet unseeing, made him unpopular with the women servants.

Nevertheless, women had a certain fascination for him: he would stare at the pretty young maids with an intent blank stare when they were not looking. Yet he was rather overbearing, domineering with them, and they resented him. It was evident to Lou that he looked upon himself as belonging to the master, not to the servant class. When he flirted with the maids, as he very often did, for he had a certain crude ostentatiousness, he seemed to let them feel that he despised them as inferiors, servants, while he admired their pretty charms, as fresh, country maids.

"I'm fair nervous of that Phoenix," said Fanny, the fair-haired girl. "He makes you feel what he'd do to you if he could."

"He'd better not try with me," said Mabel. "I'd scratch his cheeky eyes out. Cheek!--for it's nothing else! He's nobody--common as they're made!"

"He makes you feel you was there for him to trample on," said Fanny.

"Mercy, you are soft! If anybody's that it's him. Oh, my, Fanny, you've no right to let a fellow make you feel like *that!* Make *them* feel that *they're* dirt, for you to trample on: which they are!"

Fanny, however, being a shy little blonde thing, wasn't good at assuming the trampling role. She was definitely nervous of Phoenix. And he enjoyed it. An invisible smile seemed to creep up his cheek-bones, and the glint moved in his eyes as he teased her. He tormented her by his very presence, as he knew.

He would come silently up when she was busy, and stand behind her perfectly still, so that she was unaware of his presence. Then, silently, he would *make* her aware. Till she glanced nervously round, and with a scream saw him.

One day Lou watched the little play. Fanny had been picking over a bowl of blackcurrants, sitting on the bench under the maple tree in a corner of the yard. She didn't look round till she had picked up her bowl to go to the kitchen. Then there was a scream and a crash.

When Lou came out, Phoenix was crouching down silently gathering up the currants, which the little maid, scarlet and trembling, was collecting into another bowl. Phoenix seemed to be smiling down his back.

"Phoenix!" said Lou. "I wish you wouldn't startle Fanny!" He looked up and she saw the glint of ridicule in his eyes.

"Who, me?" he said.

"Yes, you. You go up behind Fanny to startle her. You're not to do it."

He slowly stood erect and lapsed into his peculiar invisible silence. Only for a second his eyes glanced at Lou's, and then she saw the cold anger, the gleam of malevolence and contempt. He could not bear being commanded, or reprimanded, by a woman.

Yet it was even worse with a man.

"What's that, Lou?" said Rico, appearing all handsome and in the picture, in white flannels with an apricot silk shirt.

"I'm telling Phoenix he's not to torment Fanny!"

"Oh!"--and Rico's voice immediately became his father's, the important government official's. "Certainly *not!* Most certainly *not!*" He looked at the scattered currants and the broken bowl. Fanny melted into tears. "This, I suppose, is some of the results! Now look here, Phoenix, you're to leave the maids strictly alone. I shall ask them to report to me whenever, or if ever, you interfere with them. But I hope you *won't* interfere with them--in any way. You understand?"

As Rico became more and more Sir Harry and the government official, Lou's bones melted more and more into discomfort. Phoenix stood in his peculiar silence, the invisible smile on his cheek-bones.

"You understand what I'm saying to you?" Rico demanded, in intensified acid tones.

But Phoenix only stood there, as it were behind a cover of his own will, and looked back at Rico with a faint smile on his face and the glint moving in his eyes.

"Do you intend to answer?" Rico's upper lip lifted nastily. "Mrs. Witt is my boss," came from Phoenix.

The scarlet flew up Rico's throat and flushed his face, his eyes went glaucous. Then quickly his face turned yellow.

Lou looked at the two men: her husband, whose rages, over-controlled, were organically terrible: the half-breed, whose dark-coloured lips were widened in a faint smile of derision, but in whose eyes caution and hate were playing against one another. She realised that Phoenix would accept her reprimand, or her mother's, because he could despise the two of them as mere women. But Rico's business aroused murder pure and simple.

She took her husband's arm.

"Come, dear!" she said in her half-plaintive way. "I'm sure Phoenix understands. We all understand. Go to the kitchen, Fanny, never mind the currants.

There are plenty more in the garden."

Rico was always thankful to be drawn quickly, submissively away from his own rage. He was afraid of it. He was afraid lest he should fly at the groom in some horrible fashion. The very thought horrified him. But in actuality he came very near to it.

He walked stiffly, feeling paralysed by his own fury. And those words, *Mrs. Witt is my boss*, were like hot acid in his brain. An insult!

"By the way, Belle-Mère!" he said when they joined Mrs. Witt--she hated being called Belle-Mère, and once said: "If I'm the bell-mare, are you one of the colts?"--She also hated his voice of smothered fury--"I had to speak to Phoenix about persecuting the maids. He took the liberty of informing me that you were his boss, so perhaps you had better speak to him."

"I certainly will. I believe they're my maids, and nobody else's, so it's my duty to look after them. Who was he persecuting?"

"I'm the responsible one, mother," said Lou.

Rico disappeared in a moment. He must get out: get away from the house. How? Something was wrong with the car. Yet he must get away, away. He would go over to Corrabach. He would ride St. Mawr. He had been talking about the horse, and Flora Manby was dying to see him. She had said: "Oh, I can't *wait* to see that marvellous horse of yours."

He would ride him over. It was only seven miles. He found Lou's maid Elena, and sent her to tell Lewis. Meanwhile, to soothe himself, he dressed himself most carefully in white riding-breeches and a shirt of purple silk crepe, with a flowing black tie spotted red like a ladybird, and black riding-boots. Then he took a *chic* little white hat with a black band.

St. Mawr was saddled and waiting, and Lewis had saddled a second horse.

"Thanks, Lewis, I'm going alone!" said Rico.

This was the first time he had ridden St. Mawr in the country, and he was nervous. But he was also in the hell of a smothered fury. All his careful dressing had not really soothed him. So his fury consumed his nervousness.

He mounted with a swing, blind and rough. St. Mawr reared.

"Stop that!" snarled Rico, and put him to the gate.

Once out in the village street, the horse went dancing sideways. He insisted on dancing at the sidewalk, to the exaggerated terror of the children. Rico, exasperated, pulled him across. But no, he wouldn't go down the centre of the village street. He began dancing and edging on to the other sidewalk, so the foot-passengers fled into the shops in terror.

The devil was in him. He would turn down every turning where he was not meant to go. He reared with panic at a furniture van. He *insisted* on going down the wrong side of the road. Rico was riding him with a martingale, and he could see the rolling, bloodshot eye.

"Damn you, *go!*" said Rico, giving him a dig with the spurs. And away they went, down the high-road, in a thunderbolt. It was a hot day, with thunder threatening, so Rico was soon in a flame of heat. He held on tight, with fixed eyes, trying all the time to rein in the horse. What he really was afraid of was that the brute would shy suddenly as he galloped. Watching for this, he didn't care when they sailed past the turning to Corrabach.

St. Mawr flew on, in a sort of *élan*. Marvellous the power and life in the creature. There was really a great joy in the motion. If only he wouldn't take the corners at a gallop, nearly swerving Rico off! Luckily the road was clear. To ride, to ride at this terrific gallop, on into eternity!

After several miles, the horse slowed down, and Rico managed to pull him into a lane that might lead to Corrabach. When all was said and done, it was a wonderful ride. St. Mawr could go like the wind, but with that luxurious heavy ripple of life which is like nothing else on earth. It seemed to carry one at once into another world, away from the life of the nerves.

So Rico arrived, after all, something of a conqueror at Corrabach. To be sure, he was perspiring, and so was his horse. But he was a hero from another, heroic world.

"Oh, such a hot ride!" he said, as he walked on to the lawn at Corrabach Hall. "Between the sun and the horse, really!--between two fires!"

"Don't you trouble, you're looking dandy, a bit hot and flushed like," said Flora Manby. "Let's go and see your horse."

And he exclamation was: "Oh, he's *lovely!* He's fine! I'd love to try him once--"

Rico decided to accept the invitation to stay overnight at Corrabach. Usually he was very careful, and refused to stay, unless Lou was with him. But they telephoned to the post office at Chomesbury, would Mr. Jones please send a message to Lady Carrington that Sir Henry was staying the night at Corrabach Hall, but would be home next day. Mr. Jones received the request with unction, and said he would go over himself to give the message to Lady Carrington.

Lady Carrington was in the walled garden. The peculiarity of Mrs. Witt's house was that, for grounds proper, it had the churchyard.

"I never thought, Louise, that one day I should have an old English churchyard for my lawns and shrubbery and park, and funeral mourners for my herds of deer. It's curious. For the first time in my life a funeral has become a real thing to me. I feel I could write a book on them."

But Louise only felt intimidated.

At the back of the house was a flagged courtyard, with stables and a maple tree in a corner, and big doors opening on to the village street. But at the side was a walled garden, with fruit trees and currant bushes and a great bed of rhubarb, and some tufts of flowers, peonies, pink roses, sweet williams. Phoenix, who had a certain taste for gardening, would be out there thinning the carrots or tying up the lettuce. He was not lazy. Only he would not take work seriously, as a job. He would be quite amused tying up lettuces, and would tie up head after head, quite prettily. Then, becoming bored, he would abandon his task, light a cigarette, and go and stand on the threshold of the big doors, in full view of the street, watching, and yet completely indifferent.

After Rico's departure on St. Mawr, Lou went into the garden. And there she saw Phoenix working in the onion-bed. He was bending over, in his own silence, busy with nimble, amused fingers among the grassy young onions. She thought he had not seen her, so she went down another path to where a swing bed hung under the apple tree. There she sat with a book and a bundle of magazines. But she did not read.

She was musing vaguely. Vaguely, she was glad that Rico was away for a while. Vaguely, she felt a sense of bitterness, of complete futility: the complete futility of her living. This left her drifting in a sea of utter chagrin. And Rico seemed to her the symbol of the futility. Vaguely, she was aware that something else existed, but she didn't know where it was or what it was.

In the distance she could see Phoenix's dark, rather tall-built head, with its black, fine, intensely-living hair tending to stand on end, like a brush with long, very fine black bristles. His hair, she thought, betrayed him as an animal of a different species. He was growing a little bored by weeding onions: that also she could tell. Soon he would want some other amusement.

Presently Lewis appeared. He was small, energetic, a little bit bow-legged, and he walked with a slight strut. He wore khaki riding-breeches, leather gaiters, and a blue shirt. And, like Phoenix, he rarely had any cap or hat on his head. His thick black hair was parted at the side and brushed over heavily sideways, dropping on his forehead at the right. It was very long, a real mop, under which his eyebrows were dark and steady.

"Seen Lady Carrington?" he asked of Phoenix.

"Yes, she's sitting on that swing over there--she's been there quite a while."

The wretch--he had seen her from the very first!

Lewis came striding over, looking towards her with his pale-grey eyes, from under his mop of hair.

"Mr. Jones from the post office wants to see you, my Lady, with a message from Sir Henry."

Instantly alarm took possession of Lou's soul.

"Oh!--Does he want to see me personally?--What message? Is anything wrong?"--And her voice trailed out over the last word, with a sort of anxious nonchalance.

"I don't think it's anything amiss," said Lewis reassuringly.

"Oh! You don't," the relief came into her voice. Then she looked at Lewis with a slight, winning smile in her unmatched eyes. "I'm so afraid of St. Mawr, you know." Her voice was soft and cajoling. Phoenix was listening in the distance.

"St. Mawr's all right, if you don't do nothing to him," Lewis replied.

"I'm sure he is!--But how is one to know when one is doing something to him?--Tell Mr. Jones to come here, please," she concluded, on a changed tone.

Mr. Jones, a man of forty-five, thick-set, with a fresh complexion and rather foolish brown eyes, and a big brown moustache, came prancing down the path, smiling rather fatuously, and doffing his straw hat with a gorgeous bow the moment he saw Lou sitting in her slim white frock on the coloured swing bed under the trees with their hard green apples.

"Good-morning, Mr. Jones!"

"Good-morning, Lady Carrington.--If I may say so, what a picture you make--a beautiful picture--"

He beamed under his big brown moustache like the greatest lady-killer.

"Do I!--Did Sir Henry say he was all right?"

"He didn't *say* exactly, but I should expect he is all right--" and Mr. Jones delivered his message, in the mayonnaise of his own unction.

"Thank you so much, Mr. Jones. It's awfully good of you to come and tell me. Now I shan't worry about Sir Henry *at all*."

"It's a great pleasure to come and deliver a satisfactory message to Lady Carrington. But it won't be kind to Sir Henry if you don't worry about him *at all* in his absence. We all enjoy being worried about by those we love--so long as there is nothing to worry about, of course!"

"Quite!" said Lou. "Now won't you take a glass of port and a biscuit, or a whisky and soda? And thank you ever so much."

"Thank you, my Lady. I might drink a whisky and soda, since you are so good."

And he beamed fatuously.

"Let Mr. Jones mix himself a whisky and soda, Lewis," said Lou.

"Heavens!" she thought, as the postmaster retreated a little uncomfortably down the garden path, his bald spot passing in and out of the sun, under the trees: "How ridiculous everything is, how ridiculous, ridiculous!" Yet she didn't really dislike Mr. Jones and his interlude.

Phoenix was melting away out of the garden. He had to follow the fun.

"Phoenix!" Lou called. "Bring me a glass of water, will you? Or send somebody with it."

He stood in the path looking round at her.

"All right!" he said

And he turned away again.

She did not like being alone in the garden. She liked to have the men working somewhere near. Curious how pleasant it was to sit there in the garden when

Phoenix was about, or Lewis. It made her feel she could never be lonely or jumpy. But when Rico was there, she was all aching nerve.

Phoenix came back with a glass of water, lemon juice, sugar, and a small bottle of brandy. He knew Lou liked a spoonful of brandy in her iced lemonade.

"How thoughtful of you, Phoenix!" she said. "Did Mr. Jones get his whisky?"

"He was just getting it."

"That's right.--By the way, Phoenix, I wish you wouldn't get mad if Sir Henry speaks to you. He is *really* so kind."

She looked up at the man. He stood there watching her in silence, the invisible smile on his face, and the inscrutable Indian glint moving in his eyes. What was he thinking? There was something passive and almost submissive about him, but underneath this, an unyielding resistance and cruelty: yes, even cruelty. She felt that, on top, he was submissive and attentive, bringing her her lemonade as she liked it, without being told: thinking for her quite subtly. But underneath there was an unchanging hatred. He submitted circumstantially, he worked for a wage. And even circumstantially, he *liked* his mistress--*la patrona*--and her daughter. But much deeper than any circumstance or any circumstantial liking, was the categorical hatred upon which he was founded, and with which he was powerless. His liking for Lou and for Mrs. Witt, his serving them and working for a wage, was all side-tracking his own nature, which was grounded on hatred of their very existence. But what was he to do? He had to live. Therefore he had to serve, to work for a wage, and even to be faithful.

And yet *their* existence made his own existence negative. If he was to exist, positively, they would have to cease to exist. At the same time, a fatal sort of tolerance made him serve these women, and go on serving.

"Sir Henry is so kind to everybody," Lou insisted.

The half-breed met her eyes, and smiled uncomfortably. "Yes, he's a kind man," he replied, as if sincerely. "Then why do you mind if he speaks to you?"

"I don't mind," said Phoenix glibly.

"But you do. Or else you wouldn't make him so angry."

"Was he angry? I don't know," said Phoenix.

"He was very angry. And you *do* know."

"No, I don't know if he's angry. I don't know," the fellow persisted. And there was a glib sort of satisfaction in his tone.

"That's awfully unkind of you, Phoenix," she said, growing offended in her turn.

"No, I don't know if he's angry. I don't want to make him angry. I don't know--"

He had taken on a tone of naïve ignorance, which at once gratified her pride as a woman, and deceived her.

"Well, you believe me when I tell you you *did* make him angry, don't you?"

"Yes, I believe when you tell me."

"And you promise me, won't you, not to do it again? It's so bad for him--so bad for his nerves, and for his eyes. It makes them inflamed, and injures his eyesight. And you know, as an artist, it's terrible if anything happens to his eyesight--"

Phoenix was watching her closely, to take it in. He still was not good at understanding continuous, logical statement. Logical connection in speech seemed to stupefy him, make him stupid. He understood in disconnected assertions of fact. But he had gathered what she said. "He gets mad at you. When he gets mad, it hurts his eyes. His eyes hurt him. He can't see, because his eyes hurt him. He wants to paint a picture, he can't. He can't paint a picture, he can't see clear--"

Yes, he had understood. She saw he had understood. The bright glint of satisfaction moved in his eyes.

"So now promise me, won't you, you won't make him mad again: you won't make him angry?"

"No, I won't make him angry. I don't do anything to make him angry," Phoenix answered, rather glibly.

"And you do understand, don't you? You do know how kind he is: how he'd do a good, turn to anybody?"

"Yes, he's a kind man," said Phoenix.

"I'm so glad you realise. There, that's luncheon! How nice It is to sit here in the garden, when everybody is nice to you! No, I can carry the tray, don't you bother."

But he took the tray from her hand and followed her to the house. And as he walked behind her, he watched the slim white nape of her neck, beneath the clustering of her bobbed hair, something as a stoat watches a rabbit he is following.

In the afternoon Lou retreated once more to her place in the garden. There she lay, sitting with a bunch of pillows behind her, neither reading nor working, just musing. She had learned the new joy: to do absolutely nothing, but to lie and let the sunshine filter through the leaves, to see the bunch of red-hot-poker flowers pierce scarlet into the afternoon, beside the comparative neutrality of some foxgloves. The mere colour of hard red, like the big Oriental poppies that had fallen, and these poker flowers, lingered in her consciousness like a communication.

Into this peaceful indolence, when even the big, dark-grey tower of the church beyond the wall and the yew trees was keeping its bells in silence, advanced Mrs. Witt, in a broad Panama hat and a white dress.

"Don't you want to ride, or do something, Louise?" she asked ominously.

"Don't you want to be peaceful, mother?" retorted Louise.

"Yes--an *active* peace.--I can't *believe* that my daughter can be content to lie on a hammock and do nothing, not even read or improve her mind, the greater part of the day."

"Well, your daughter is content to do that. It's her greatest pleasure."

"I know it. I can see it. And it surprises me very much. When I was your age, I was never still. I had so much *go*--"

"Those maids, thank God,

Are 'neath the sod,

And all the generation."

"No, but, mother, I only take life differently. Perhaps you used up that sort of *go*. I'm the harem type, mother: only I never want the men inside the lattice."

"Are you really my daughter?--Well! A woman never knows what will happen to her. I'm an *American* woman, and I suppose I've got to remain one, no matter where I am.--What did you want, Lewis?"

The groom had approached down the path.

"If I am to saddle Poppy?" said Lewis.

"No, apparently not!" replied Mrs. Witt. "Your mistress prefers the hammock to the saddle."

"Thank you, Lewis. What mother says is true this afternoon, at least." And she gave him a peculiar little cross-eyed smile.

"Who," said Mrs. Witt to the man, "has been cutting at your hair?"

There was a moment of silent resentment.

"I did it myself, Mam! Sir Henry said it was too long."

"He certainly spoke the truth. But I believe there's a barber in the village on Saturdays--or you could ride over to Shrewsbury. Just turn round, and let me look at the back. Is it the money?"

"No, Mam. I don't like these fellows touching my head." He spoke coldly, with a certain hostile reserve that at once piqued Mrs. Witt.

"Don't you really!" she said. "But it's quite *impossible* for you to go about as you are. It gives you a half-witted appearance. Go now into the yard and get a chair and a dust-sheet. I'll cut your hair."

The man hesitated, hostile.

"Don't be afraid, I know how it's done. I've cut the hair of many a poor wounded boy in hospital: and shaved them too. *You've got such a touch, nurse!* Poor fellow, he was dying, though none of us knew it.--Those are the compliments I value, Louise.--Get that chair now, and a dust-sheet, I'll borrow your hair-scissors from Elena, Louise."

Mrs. Witt, happily on the war-path, was herself again. She didn't care for work, actual work. But she loved trimming. She loved arranging unnatural and pretty salads, devising new and piquant-looking ice-creams, having a turkey stuffed exactly as she knew a stuffed turkey in Louisiana, with chestnuts and butter and stuff, or showing a servant how to turn waffles on a waffle-iron, or to bake a ham with brown sugar and cloves and a moistening of rum. She liked pruning rose trees, or beginning to cut a yew hedge into shape. She liked ordering her own and Louise's shoes, with an exactitude and a knowledge of shoe-making that sent the salesmen crazy. She was a demon in shoes. Reappearing from America, she would pounce on her daughter. "Louise, throw those shoes away. Give them to one of the maids."--"But, mother, they are some of the best French shoes. I like them."--"Throw them away. A shoe has only two excuses for existing: perfect comfort or perfect appearance. Those have neither. I have brought you some shoes."--Yes, she had brought ten pairs of shoes from New York. She knew her daughter's foot as she knew her own.

So now she was in her element, looming behind Lewis as he sat in the middle of the yard swathed in a dust-sheet. She had on an overall and a pair of wash-leather gloves, and she poised a pair of long scissors like one of the Fates. In her big hat she looked curiously young, but with the youth of a bygone generation. Her heavy-lidded, laconic grey eyes were alert, studying the groom's black mop of hair. Her eyebrows made thin, uptilting black arches on her brow. Her fresh skin was slightly powdered, and she was really handsome in a bold, bygone, eighteenth-century style. Some of the curious, adventurous stoicism of the eighteenth century: and then a Certain blatant American efficiency.

Lou, who had strayed into the yard to see, looked so much younger and so many thousand of years older than her mother, as she stood in her wisp-like diffidence, the clusters of grape-like bobbed hair hanging beside her face, with its fresh colouring and its ancient weariness, her slightly squinting eyes, that were so disillusioned they were becoming faunlike.

"Not too short, mother, not too short!" she remonstrated, as Mrs. Witt, with a terrific flourish of efficiency, darted at the man's black hair, and the thick flakes fell like black snow.

"Now, Louise, I'm right in this job, please don't interfere. Two things I hate to see: a man with his wool in his neck and ears: and a bare-faced young man who looks as if he'd bought his face as well as his hair from a men's beauty-specialist."

And efficiently she bent down, clip--clip--clipping! while Lewis sat utterly immobile, with sunken head, in a sort of despair.

Phoenix stood against the stable door, with his restless, eternal cigarette. And in the kitchen doorway the maids appeared and fled, appeared and fled in delight. The old gardener, a fixture who went with the house, creaked in and stood with his legs apart, silent in intense condemnation.

"First time I ever see such a thing!" he muttered to himself, as he creaked on into the garden. He was a bad-tempered old soul, who thoroughly disapproved of the household, and would have given notice, but that he knew which side his bread was buttered: and there was butter unstinted on his bread in Mrs. Witt's kitchen.

Mrs. Witt stood back to survey her handiwork, holding those terrifying shears with their beak erect. Lewis lifted his head and looked stealthily round, like a creature in a trap. "Keep still!" she said. "I haven't finished."

And she went for his front hair, with vigour, lifting up long layers and snipping off the ends artistically: till at last he sat with a black aureole upon the floor, and his ears standing out with curious new alertness from the sides of his clean-clipped head.

"Stand up," she said, "and let me look."

He stood up, looking absurdly young, with the hair all cut away from his neck and ears, left thick only on top. She surveyed her work with satisfaction.

"You look so much younger," she said, "you would be surprised. Sit down again."

She clipped the back of his neck with the shears, and then, with a very slight hesitation, she said:

"Now about the beard!"

But the man rose suddenly from the chair, pulling the dust-cloth from his neck with desperation.

"No, I'll do that myself," he said, looking her in the eyes with a cold light in his pale-grey, uncanny eyes.

She hesitated in a kind of wonder at his queer male rebellion.

"Now, listen, I shall do it much better than you--and besides," she added hurriedly, snatching at the dust-cloth he was flinging on the chair--"I haven't quite finished round the ears."

"I think I shall do," he said, again looking her in the eyes, with a cold, white gleam of finality. "Thank you for what you've done."

And he walked away to the stable.

"You'd better sweep up here," Mrs. Witt called.

"Yes, Mam," he replied, looking round at her again with an odd resentment, but continuing to walk away.

"However!" said Mrs. Witt, "I suppose he'll do."

And she divested herself of gloves and overall and walked indoors to wash and to change. Lou went indoors too.

"It is extraordinary what hair that man has!" said Mrs. Witt. "Did I tell you when I was in Paris, I saw a woman's face in the hotel that I thought I knew? I couldn't place her, till she was coming towards me. 'Aren't you Rachel Fannière?' she said. 'Aren't you Janette Leroy?' We hadn't seen each other since we were girls of twelve and thirteen, at school in New Orleans. 'Oh!' she said to me. 'Is every illusion doomed to perish? You had such wonderful golden curls! All my life I've said, Oh, if only I had such lovely hair as Rachel Fannière! I've seen those beautiful golden curls of yours all my life. And now I meet you, you're grey!' Wasn't that terrible, Louise? Well, that man's hair made me think of it--so thick and curious. It's strange what a difference there is in hair; I suppose it's because he's just an animal--no mind! There's nothing I admire in a man like a good *mind*. Your father was a very clever man, and all the men I've admired have been clever. But isn't it curious now, I've never cared much to touch their hair. How strange life is! If it gives one thing, it takes away another.--And even those poor boys in hospital: I have shaved them, or cut their hair, like a mother, never thinking anything of it. Lovely, intelligent, clean boys, most of them were. Yet it never did anything to me. I never knew before that something could happen to one from a person's *hair!* Like to Janette Leroy from my curls when I was a child. And now I'm grey, as she says.--I wonder how old a man Lewis is, Louise! Didn't he look absurdly young with his ears pricking up?"

"I think Rico said he was forty or forty-one."

"And never been married?"

"No--not as far as I know."

"Isn't that curious now!--just an animal! No mind! A man with no mind! I've always thought that the *most* despicable thing. Yet such wonderful hair to touch. Your Henry has quite a good mind, yet I would simply shrink from touching his hair. I suppose one likes stroking a cat's fur, just the same. Just the animal in man. Curious that I never seem to have met it, Louise. Now I come to think of it, he has the eyes of a human cat: a human tom-cat. Would you call him stupid? Yes, he's very stupid."

"No, mother, he's not stupid. He only doesn't care about most things."

"Like an animal! But what a strange look he has in his eyes! A strange sort of intelligence! and a confidence in himself. Isn't that curious, Louise, in a man with as little mind as he has? Do you know, I should say he could see through a woman pretty well."

"Why, mother!" said Lou impatiently. "I think one gets so tired of your men with mind, as you call it. There are so many of that sort of clever men. And there are lots of men who aren't very clever, but are rather nice: and lots are stupid. It seems to me there's something else besides mind and cleverness, or niceness or cleanness. Perhaps it is the animal. Just think of St. Mawr! I've thought so much about him. We call him an animal, but we never know what it means. He seems a far greater mystery to me than a clever man. He's a horse. Why can't one say in the same way of a man: 'He's a man?' There seems no mystery in being a man. But there's a terrible mystery in St. Mawr."

Mrs. Witt watched her daughter quizzically.

"Louise," she said, "you won't tell me that the mere animal is all that counts in a man. I will never believe it. Man is wonderful because he is able to think."

"But is he?" cried Lou, with sudden exasperation. "Their thinking seems to me all so childish: like stringing the same beads over and over again. Ah, men! They and their thinking are all so *paltry*. How can you be impressed?"

Mrs. Witt raised her eyebrows sardonically.

"Perhaps I'm not--any more," she said with a grim smile.

"But," she added, "I still can't see that I am to be impressed by the mere animal in man. The animals are the same as we are. It seems to me they have the same feelings and wants as we do in a commonplace way. The only difference is that they have no minds: no human minds, at least. And no matter what you say, Louise, lack of minds makes the commonplace."

Lou knitted her brows nervously.

"I suppose it does, mother.--But men's minds are so commonplace: look at Dean Vyner and his mind! Or look at Arthur Balfour, as a shining example. Isn't *that* commonplace, that cleverness? I would hate St. Mawr to be spoilt by such a mind."

"Yes, Louise, so would I. Because the men you mention are really old women, knitting the same pattern over and over again. Nevertheless, I shall never alter my belief that real mind is all that matters in a man, and it's that *that* we women love."

"Yes, mother!--But what *is* real mind? The old woman who knits the most complicated pattern? Oh, I can hear all their needles clicking, the clever men! As a matter of fact, mother, I believe Lewis has far more real mind than Dean Vyner or any of the clever ones. He has a good intuitive mind, he knows things without thinking them."

"That may be, Louise! But he is a servant. He is *under*. A real man should never be under. And then you could never be intimate with a man like Lewis."/

"I don't want intimacy, mother. I'm too tired of it all. I love St. Mawr because he isn't intimate. He stands where one can't get at him. And he burns with life. And where does his life come from, to him? That's the mystery. That great burning life in him, which never is dead. Most men have a deadness in them, that frightens me so, because of my own deadness. Why can't men get their life straight, like St. Mawr, and then think? Why can't they think quick, mother: quick as a woman: only farther than we do? Why isn't men's thinking quick like fire, mother? Why is it so slow, so dead, so deadly dull?"

"I can't tell you, Louise. My own opinion of the men of to-day has grown very small. But I can live in spite of it."

"No, mother. We seemed to be living off old fuel, like the camel when he lives off his hump. Life doesn't rush into us, as it does even into St. Mawr, and he's a dependent animal. I can't live, mother. I just can't."

"I don't see why not! *I'm* full of life."

"I know you are, mother. But I'm not, and I'm your daughter.--And don't misunderstand me, mother! I don't want to be an animal like a horse or a cat or a lioness, though they all fascinate me, the way they get their life *straight*, not from a lot of old tanks, as we do. I don't admire the caveman, and that sort of thing. But think, mother, if we could get our lives straight from the source, as the animals do, and still be ourselves. You don't like men yourself. But you've no idea how men just tire me out: even the very thought of them. You say they are too animal. But they're not, mother. It's the animal in them has gone perverse, or cringing, or humble, or domesticated, like dogs. I don't know one single man who is a proud living animal. I know they've left off really thinking. But then men always do leave off really thinking when the last bit of wild animal dies in them."

"Because we have minds--"

"We have no minds once we are tame, mother. Men are all women, knitting and crocheting words together."

"I can't altogether agree, you know, Louise."

"I know you don't.--You like clever men. But clever men are mostly such *unpleasant* animals. As animals, so very unpleasant. And in men like Rico, the animal has gone queer and wrong. And in those nice clean boys you liked so much in the war, there is no wild animal left in them. They're all tame dogs, even when they're brave and well-bred. They're all tame dogs, mother, with human masters. There's no mystery in them."

"What do you want, Louise? You do want the cave man, who'll knock you on the head with a club."

"Don't be silly, mother. That's much more your subconscious line, you admirer of Mind--I don't consider the cave man is a real human animal at all. He's a brute, a degenerate. A pure animal man would be as lovely as a deer or a leopard, burning like a flame fed straight from underneath. And he'd be part of the unseen, like a mouse is, even. And he'd never cease to wonder, he'd breathe silence and unseen wonder, as the partridges do, running in the stubble. He'd be all the animals in turn, instead of one, fixed, automatic thing, which he is now, grinding on the nerves.--Ah, no, mother, I want the wonder back again, or I shall die. I don't want to be like you, just criticising and annihilating these dreary people, and enjoying it."

"My dear daughter, whatever else the human animal might be, he'd be a dangerous commodity."

"I wish he would, mother. I'm dying of these empty danger-less men, who are only sentimental and spiteful."

"Nonsense, you're not dying."

"I am, mother. And I should be dead if there weren't St. Mawr and Phoenix and Lewis in the world."

"St. Mawr and Phoenix and Lewis! I thought you said they were servants."

"That's the worst of it. If only they were masters! If only there were some men with as much natural life as they have, and their brave, quick minds that commanded instead of serving!"

"There are no such men," said Mrs. Witt, with a certain grim satisfaction.

"I know it. But I'm young, and I've got to live. And the thing that is offered me as life just starves me, starves me to death, mother. What am I to do? You enjoy shattering people like Dean Vyner. But I am young, I can't live that way!"

"That may be."

It had long ago struck Lou how much more her mother realised and understood than ever Rico did. Rico was afraid, always afraid of realising. Rico, with his good manners and his habitual kindness, and that peculiar imprisoned sneer of his.

He arrived home next morning on St. Mawr, rather flushed and gaudy, and over-kind, with an empressé anxiety about Lou's welfare which spoke too many volumes. Especially as he was accompanied by Flora Manby, and by Flora's sister Elsie, and Elsie's husband, Frederick Edwards. They all came on horseback.

"Such awful ages since I saw you!" said Flora to Lou. "Sorry if we burst in on you. We're only just saying 'How do you do!' and going on to the inn. They've got rooms all ready for us there. We thought we'd stay just one night over here, and ride to-morrow to the Devil's Chair. Won't you come? Lots of fun! Isn't Mrs. Witt at home?"

Mrs. Witt was out for the moment. When she returned she had on her curious stiff face, yet she greeted the newcomers with a certain cordiality: she felt it would be diplomatic, no doubt.

"There *are* two rooms here," she said, "and if you care to poke into them, why, we shall be *delighted* to have you. But I'll show them to you first, because they are poor, inconvenient rooms, with no running water and *miles* from the baths."

Flora and Elsie declared that they were "perfectly darling sweet rooms--not overcrowded."

"Well," said Mrs. Witt, "the conveniences certainly don't fill up much space. But if you like to take them for what they are--"

"Why, we feel absolutely overwhelmed, don't we, Elsie?--But we've no clothes--!"

Suddenly the silence had turned into a house-party. The Manby girls appeared to lunch in fine muslin dresses, bought in Paris, fresh as daisies. Women's clothing takes up so little space, especially in summer! Fred Edwards was one of those blond Englishmen with a little brush moustache and those strong blue eyes which were always attempting the sentimental, but which Lou, in her prejudice, considered cruel: upon what grounds she never analysed. However, he took a gallant tone with her at once, and she had to seem to simper. Rico, watching her, was so relieved when he saw the simper coming.

It had begun again, the whole clockwork of 'lots of fun'!

"Isn't Fred flirting perfectly outrageously with Lady Carrington!--She looks so *sweet!*" cried Flora, over her coffee-cup. "Don't you mind, Harry!"

They called Rico 'Harry'! His boy-name.

"Only a very little," said Harry. "*L'uomo è cacciatore.*"

"Oh, now, what does that mean?" cried Flora, who always thrilled to Rico's bits of affectation.

"It means," said Mrs. Witt, leaning forward and speaking in her most suave voice, "that man is a hunter."

Even Flora shrank under the smooth acid of the irony. "Oh, well now!" she cried. "If he is, then what is woman?"

"The hunted," said Mrs. Witt, in a still smoother acid. "At least," said Rico, "she is always *game!*"

"Ah, is she though!" came Fred's manly, well-bred tones. "I'm not so sure."

Mrs. Witt looked from one man to the other, as if she were dropping them down the bottomless pit.

Lou escaped to look at St. Mawr. He was still moist where the saddle had been. And he seemed a little bit extinguished, as if virtue had gone out of him.

But when he lifted his lovely naked head, like a bunch of flames, to see who it was had entered, she saw he was still himself. Forever sensitive and alert, his head lifted like the summit of a fountain. And within him the clean bones striking to the earth, his hoofs intervening between him and the ground like lesser jewels.

He knew her and did not resent her. But he took no notice of her. He would never 'respond'. At first she had resented It. Now she was glad. He would never be intimate, thank heaven.

She hid herself away till tea-time, but she could not hide from the sound of voices. Dinner was early, at seven. Dean Vyner came--Mrs. Vyner was an invalid--and also an artist who had a studio in the village and did etchings. He was a man of about thirty-eight, and poor, just beginning to accept himself as a failure, as far as making money goes. But he worked at his etchings and studied esoteric matters like astrology and alchemy. Rico patronised him, and was a little afraid of him. Lou could not quite make him out. After knocking about Paris and London and Munich, he was trying to become staid, and to persuade himself that English village life, with squire and dean in the background, humble artist in the middle, and labourer in the common foreground, was a genuine life. His self-persuasion was only moderately successful. This was betrayed by the curious arrest in his body: he seemed to have to force himself into movements: and by the curious duplicity in his yellow-grey, twinkling eyes, that twinkled and expanded like a goat's, with mockery, irony, and frustration.

"Your face is curiously like Pan's," said Lou to him at dinner.

It was true, in a commonplace sense. He had the tilted eyebrows, the twinkling goaty look, and the pointed ears of a goat-Pan.

"People have said so," he replied. "But I'm afraid it's not the face of the Great God Pan. Isn't it rather the Great Goat Pan!"

"I say, that's good!" cried Rico. "The Great Goat Pan!"

"I have always found it difficult," said the Dean, "to see the Great God Pan in that goat-legged old father of satyrs. He may have a good deal of influence--the world will always be full of goaty old satyrs. But we find them somewhat vulgar. The goaty old satyrs are too comprehensible to me to be venerable, and I fail to see a Great God in the father of them all."

"Your ears should be getting red," said Lou to Cartwright. She, too, had an odd squinting smile that suggested nymphs. so irresponsible and unbelieving.

"Oh no, nothing personal!" cried the Dean.

"I am not sure," said Cartwright, with a small smile. "But don't you imagine Pan once was a great god before the anthropomorphic Greeks turned him into half a man?"

"Ah!--maybe. This is very possible. But--I have noticed the limitation in my-self--my mind has no grasp whatsoever of Europe before the Greeks arose. Mr. Wells's Outline does not help me there, either," the Dean added with a smile.

"But what was Pan before he was a man with goat legs?" asked Lou.

"Before he looked like me!" said Cartwright, with a faint grin. "I should say he was the god that is hidden in everything. In those days you saw the thing, you never saw the god in it: I mean in the tree or the fountain or the animal. If you ever saw the God instead of the thing, you died. If you saw it with the naked eye, that is. But in the night you might see the God. And you knew it was there."

"The modern pantheist not only sees the God in everything, he takes photo-graphs of it," said the Dean.

"Oh, and the divine pictures he paints!" cried Rico.

"Quite!" said Cartwright.

"But if they never *saw* the God in the thing, the old ones, how did they know he was there? How did they have any Pan at all?" said Lou.

"Pan was the hidden mystery--the hidden cause. That's how it was a Great God. Pan wasn't he at all: not even a great God. He was Pan. All: what you see when you see in full. In the day-time you see the thing. But if your third eye is open, which sees only the things that can't be seen, you may see Pan within the thing, hidden: you may see with your third eye, which is darkness."

"Do you think I might see Pan in a horse, for example?"

"Easily. In St. Mawr!"--Cartwright gave her a knowing look.

"But," said Mrs. Witt, "it would be difficult, I should say, to open the third eye and see Pan in a man."

"Probably," said Cartwright, smiling. "In man he is over-visible: the old satyr: the fallen Pan."

"Exactly!" said Mrs. Witt. And she fell into a muse. "The fallen Pan!" she re-echoed. "Wouldn't a man be wonderful in whom Pan hadn't fallen!"

Over the coffee in the grey drawing-room she suddenly asked:

"Supposing, Mr. Cartwright, one *did* open the third eye and see Pan in an ac-tual man--I wonder what it would be like?"

She half lowered her eyelids and tilted her face in a strange way, as if she were tasting something, and not quite sure.

"I wonder!" he said, smiling his enigmatic smile. But she could see he did not understand.

"Louise!" said Mrs. Witt at bed-time. "Come into my room for a moment, I want to ask you something."

"What is it, mother?"

"You, you get something from what Mr. Cartwright said about seeing Pan with the third eye? Seeing Pan in something?"

Mrs. Witt came rather close and tilted her face with strange insinuating question at her daughter.

"I think I do, mother."

"In what?"--The question came as a pistol-shot.

"I think, mother," said Lou reluctantly, "in St. Mawr."

"In a horse!"--Mrs. Witt contracted her eyes slightly. "Yes, I can see that. I know what you mean. It *is* in St. Mawr. It *is!* But in St. Mawr it makes me *afraid*--" she dragged out the word. Then she came a step closer. "But, Louise, did you ever see it in a man?"

"What, mother?"

"Pan. Did you ever see Pan in a man, as you see Pan in St. Mawr?"

Louise hesitated.

"No, mother, I don't think I did. When I look at men with my third eye, as you call it--I think I see--mostly--a sort of--pancake." She uttered the last word with a despairing grin, not knowing quite what to say.

"Oh, Louise, isn't that it! Doesn't one always see a pancake! Now listen, Louise. Have you ever been in love?"

"Yes, as far as I understand it."

"Listen, now. Did you ever see Pan in the man you loved? Tell me if you did."

"As I see Pan in St. Mawr?--no, mother!" And suddenly her lips began to tremble and the tears came to her eyes.

"Listen, Louise. I've been in love innumerable times--and *really* in love twice. Twice!--yet for fifteen years I've left off wanting to have anything to do with a man, really. For fifteen years! And why? Do you know? Because I couldn't see that peculiar hidden Pan in any of them. And I became that I needed to. I needed it. But it wasn't there. Not in any man. Even when I was in love with a man, it was for other things: because I *understood* him so well, or he understood me, or we had such sympathy. Never the hidden Pan. Do you understand what I mean? Unfallen Pan!"

"More or less, mother."

"But now my third eye is coming open, I believe. I am tired of all these men like breakfast cakes, with a teaspoonful of mind or a teaspoonful of spirit in them, for baking-powder. Isn't it extraordinary: that young man Cartwright talks about Pan, but he knows nothing of it all. He knows nothing of the unfallen Pan: only the fallen Pan with goat legs and a leer--and that sort of power, don't you know."

"But what do you know of the unfallen Pan, mother?"

"Don't ask me, Louise! I feel all of a tremble, as if I was just on the verge."

She flashed a little look of incipient triumph, and said goodnight.

An excursion on horseback had been arranged for the next day, to two old groups of rocks, called the Angel's Chair and the Devil's Chair, which crowned the moor-like hills looking into Wales, ten miles away. Everybody was going--they were to start early in the morning, and Lewis would be the guide, since no one exactly knew the way.

Lou got up soon after sunrise. There was a summer scent in the trees of early morning, and monkshood flowers stood up dark and tall, with shadows. She dressed in the green linen riding-skirt her maid had put ready for her, with a close bluish smock.

"Are you going out already, dear?" called Rico from his room.

"Just to smell the roses before we start, Rico."

He appeared in the doorway in his yellow silk pyjamas. His large blue eyes had that rolling, irritable look and the slightly bloodshot whites which made her want to escape.

"Booted and spurred!--the *energy!*" he cried.

"It's a lovely day to ride," she said.

"A lovely day to do anything *except* ride!" he said. "Why spoil the day riding?"--A curious bitter acid escaped into his tone. It was evident he hated the excursion.

"Why, we needn't go if you don't want to, Rico."

"Oh, I'm sure I shall love it, once I get started. It's all this business of *starting*, with horses and paraphernalia--"

Lou went into the yard. The horses were drinking at the trough under the pump, their colours strong and rich in the shadow of the tree.

"You're not coming with us, Phoenix?" she said. "Lewis, he's riding my horse."

She could tell Phoenix did not like being left behind.

By half-past seven everybody was ready. The sun was in the yard, the horses were saddled. They came swishing their tails. Lewis brought out St. Mawr from his separate box, speaking to him very quietly in Welsh: a murmuring, soothing little speech. Lou, alert, could see that he was uneasy. "How is St. Mawr this morning?" she asked.

"He's all right. He doesn't like so many people. He'll be all right once he's started."

The strangers were in the saddle: they moved out to the deep shade of the village road outside. Rico came to his horse to mount. St. Mawr jumped away as if he had seen the devil. "Steady, fool!" cried Rico.

The bay stood with his four feet spread, his neck arched, his big dark eye glancing sideways with that watchful, frightening look.

"You shouldn't be irritable with him, Rico!" said Lou. "Steady then, St. Mawr! Be steady."

But a certain anger rose also in her. The creature was so big, so brilliant, and so stupid, standing there with his hind legs spread, ready to jump aside or to rear terrifically, and his great eye glancing with a sort of suspicious frenzy. What was there to be suspicious of, after all?--Rico would do him no harm.

"No one will harm you, St. Mawr," she reasoned, a bit exasperated.

The groom was talking quietly, murmuringly, in Welsh. Rico was slowly advancing again to put his foot in the stirrup. The stallion was watching from the corner of his eye, a strange glare of suspicious frenzy burning stupidly. Any moment his immense physical force might be let loose in a frenzy of panic--or malice. He was really very irritating.

"Probably he doesn't like that apricot shirt," said Mrs. Witt, "although it tones into him wonderfully well."

She pronounced it *ap*-ricot, and it irritated Rico terribly. "Ought we to have *asked* him before we put it on?" he flashed, his upper lip lifting venomously.

"I should say you should," replied Mrs. Witt coolly.

Rico turned with a sudden rush to the horse. Back went the great animal, with a sudden splashing crash of hoofs on the cobble-stones, and Lewis hanging on like a shadow. Up went the forefeet, showing the belly.

"The thing is accursed," said Rico, who had dropped the reins in sudden shock, and stood marooned. His rage overwhelmed him like a black flood.

"Nothing in the world is so irritating as a horse that is acting up," thought Lou.

"Say, Harry!" called Flora from the road. "Come out here into the road to mount him."

Lewis looked at Rico and nodded. Then soothing the big, quivering animal, he led him springily out to the road under the trees, where the three friends were waiting. Lou and her mother got quickly into the saddle to follow. And in another moment Rico was mounted and bouncing down the road in the wrong direction, Lewis following on the chestnut. It was some time before Rico could get St. Mawr round. Watching him from behind, those waiting could judge how the young baronet hated it.

But at last they set off--Rico ahead, unevenly but quietly, with the two Manby girls, Lou following with the fair young man who had been in a cavalry regiment and who kept looking round for Mrs. Witt.

"Don't look round for me," she called. "I'm riding behind, out of the dust."

Just behind Mrs. Witt came Lewis. It was a whole cavalcade trotting in the morning sun past the cottages and the cottage gardens, round the field that was the recreation-ground, into the deep hedges of the lane.

"Why is St. Mawr so bad at starting? Can't you get him Into better shape?" she asked over her shoulder.

"Beg your pardon, Mam!"

Lewis trotted a little nearer. She glanced over her shoulder at him, at his dark, unmoved face, his cool little figure. "I think Mani is so ugly. Why not leave it out!" she said. Then she repeated her question.

"St. Mawr doesn't trust anybody," Lewis replied. "Not you?"

"Yes, he trusts me--mostly."

"Then why not other people?"

"They're different."

"All of them?"

"About all of them."

"How are they different?"

He looked at her with his remote, uncanny grey eyes.

"Different," he said, not knowing how else to put it.

They rode on slowly, up the steep rise of the wood, then down into a glade where ran a little railway built for hauling some mysterious mineral out of the hill in war-time, and now already abandoned. Even on this countryside the dead hand of the war lay like a corpse decomposing.

They rode up again, past the foxgloves under the trees. Ahead the brilliant St. Mawr and the sorrel and grey horses were swimming like butterflies through the sea of bracken, glittering from sun to shade, shade to sun. Then once more they were on a crest, and through the thinning trees could see the slopes of the moors beyond the next dip.

Soon they were in the open, rolling hills, golden in the morning and empty save for a couple of distant bilberry-pickers, whitish figures pick--pick--picking with curious, rather disgusting assiduity. The horses were on an old trail which climbed through the pinky tips of heather and ling, across patches of green bilberry. Here and there were tufts of harebells blue as bubbles.

They were out, high on the hills. And there to west lay Wales, folded in crumpled folds, goldish in the morning light, with its moor-like slopes and patches of corn uncannily distinct. Between was a hollow, wide valley of summer haze, showing white farms among trees, and grey slate roofs.

"Ride beside me," she said to Lewis. "Nothing makes me want to go back to America like the old look of these little villages.--You have never been to America?"

"No, Mam."

"Don't you ever want to go?"

"I wouldn't mind going."

"But you're not just crazy to go?"

"No, Mam."

"Quite content as you are?"

He looked at her, and his pale, remote eyes met hers. "I don't fret myself," he replied.

"Not about anything at all--ever?"

His eyes glanced ahead, at the other riders.

"No, Mam!" he replied, without looking at her.

She rode a few moments in silence.

"What is that over there?" she asked, pointing across the valley. "What is it called?"

"Yon's Montgomery."

"Montgomery! And is that *Wales*--?" she trailed the ending curiously.

"Yes, Mam."

"Where you come from?"

"No, Mam! I come from Merioneth."

"Not from Wales? I thought you were Welsh?"

"Yes, Mam. Merioneth *is* Wales."

"And you are Welsh?"

"Yes, Mam."

"I had a Welsh grandmother. But I come from Louisiana, and when I go back home, the negroes still call me Miss Rachel. 'Oh, my, it's little Miss Rachel come back home! Why, ain't I mighty glad to see you--u, Miss Rachel!' That gives me such a strange feeling, you know."

The man glanced at her curiously, especially when she imitated the negroes.

"Do you feel strange when you go home?" she asked.

"I was brought up by an aunt and uncle," he said. "I never want to see them."

"And you don't have any home?"

"No, Mam."

"No wife nor anything?"

"No, Mam."

"But what do you do with your life?"

"I keep to myself."

"And care about nothing?"

"I mind St. Mawr."

"But you've not always had St. Mawr--and you won't always have him.--Were you in the war?"

"Yes, Mam."

"At the front?"

"Yes, Mam--but I was a groom."

"And you came out all right?"

"I lost my little finger from a bullet."

He held up his small, dark left hand, from which the little finger was missing.

"And did you like the war--or didn't you?"

"I didn't like it."

Again his pale grey eyes met hers, and they looked so nonhuman and uncommunicative, so without connection, and inaccessible, she was troubled.

"Tell me," she said. "Did you never want a wife and a home and children, like other men?"

"No, Mam. I never wanted a home of my own."

"Nor a wife of your own?"

"No, Mam."

"Nor children of your own?"

"No, Mam."

She reined in her horse.

"Now wait a minute," she said. "Now tell me why."

His horse came to standstill, and the two riders faced one another.

"Tell me why--I must know why you never wanted a wife and children and a home. I must know why you're not like other men."

"I never felt like it," he said. "I made my life with horses."

"Did you hate people very much? Did you have a very unhappy time as a child?"

"My aunt and uncle didn't like me, and I didn't like them."

"So you've never liked anybody?"

"Maybe not," he said. "Not to get as far as marrying them." She touched her horse and moved on.

"Isn't that curious!" she said. "I've loved people, at various times. But I don't believe I've ever liked anybody, except a few of our negroes. I don't like Louise, though she's my daughter and I love her. But I don't really *like* her.--I think you're the first person I've ever liked since I was on our plantation, and we had some very *fine* negroes.--And I think that's very curious.--Now I want to know if you like *me*."

She looked at him searchingly, but he did not answer.

"Tell me," she said. "I don't mind if you say no. But tell me if you like me. I feel I must know."

The flicker of a smile went over his face--a very rare thing with him.

"Maybe I do," he said. He was thinking that she put him on a level with a negro slave on a plantation: in his idea, negroes were still slaves. But he did not care where she put him.

"Well, I'm glad--I'm glad if you like me. Because you *don't* like most people, I know that."

They had passed the hollow where the old Aldecar Chapel hid in damp isolation, beside the ruined mill, over the stream that came down from the moors. Climbing the sharp slope, they saw the folded hills like great shut fingers, with steep, deep clefts between. On the near skyline was a bunch of rocks: and away to the right another bunch.

"Yon's the Angel's Chair," said Lewis, pointing to the nearer rocks. "And yon's the Devil's Chair, where we're going."

"Oh!" said Mrs. Witt. "And aren't we going to the Angel's Chair?"

"No, mam."

"Why not?"

"There's nothing to see there. The other's higher, and bigger, and that's where folks mostly go."

"Is that so!--They give the Devil the higher seat in this country, do they? I think they're right." And as she got no answer, she added: "You believe in the Devil, don't you?"

"I never met him," he answered evasively.

Ahead, they could see the other horses twinkling in a cavalcade up the slope, the black, the bay, the two greys and the sorrel, sometimes bunching, sometimes straggling. At a gate all waited for Mrs. Witt. The fair young man fell in beside her, and talked hunting at her. He had hunted the fox over these hills, and was vigorously excited locating the spot where the hounds first gave cry, etc.

"Really!" said Mrs. Witt. "*Really!* Is that so!"

If irony could have been condensed to prussic acid, the fair young man would have ended his life's history with his reminiscences.

They came at last, trotting in file along a narrow track between heather, along the saddle of a hill, to where the knot of pale granite suddenly cropped out. It was one of those places where the spirit of aboriginal England still lingers, the old savage England, whose last blood flows still in a few Englishmen, Welshmen, Cornishmen. The rocks, whitish with weather of all the ages, jutted against the blue August sky, heavy with age-moulded roundness.

Lewis stayed below with the horses, the party scrambled rather awkwardly, in their riding-boots, up the foot-worn boulders. At length they stood in the place called the Chair, looking west, west towards Wales, that rolled in golden folds upwards. It was neither impressive nor a very picturesque landscape: the hollow valley with farms, and then the rather bare upheaval of hills, slopes with corn and moor and pasture, rising like a barricade, seemingly high, slantingly. Yet it had a strange effect on the imagination.

"Oh, mother," said Lou, "doesn't it make you feel old, old, older than anything ever was?"

"It certainly does seem aged," said Mrs. Witt.

"It makes me want to die," said Lou. "I feel we've lasted almost too long."

"Don't say that, Lady Carrington. Why, you're a spring chicken yet: or shall I say an unopened rose-bud," remarked the fair young man.

"No," said Lou. "All these millions of ancestors have used all the life up. We're not really alive, in the sense that they were alive."

"But who?" said Rico. "Who are *they?*"

"The people who lived on these hills in the days gone by."

"But the same people still live on the hills, darling. It's just the same stock."

"No, Rico. That old fighting stock that worshipped devils among these stones--I'm sure they did--"

"But look here, do you mean they were any better than we are?" asked the fair young man.

Lou looked at him quizzically.

"We don't exist," she said, squinting at him oddly.

"I jolly well know *I* do," said the fair young man.

"I consider these days are the best ever, especially for girls," said Flora Manby. "And, anyhow, they're our own days, so I don't jolly well see the use of crying them down."

They were all silent, with the last echoes of emphatic *joie de vivre* trumpeting on the air, across the hills of Wales.

"Spoken like a brick, Flora," said Rico. "Say it again, we may not have the Devil's Chair for a pulpit next time."

"I do," reiterated Flora. "I think this is the best age there ever was for a girl to have a good time in. I read all through H. G. Wells's History, and I shut it up and thanked my stars I live in nineteen-twenty odd, not in some other beastly date when a woman had to cringe before mouldy, domineering men."

After this they turned to scramble to another part of the rocks, to the famous

Needle's Eye.

"Thank you so much, I am really better without help," said Mrs. Witt to the fair young man, as she slid downwards till a piece of grey silk stocking showed above her tall boot. But she got her toe in a safe place, and in a moment stood beside him, while he caught her arm protectingly. He might as well have caught the paw of a mountain lion protectingly.

"I should like so much to know," she said suavely, looking into his eyes with a demonish straight look, "what makes you so certain that you exist?"

He looked back at her, and his jaunty blue eyes went baffled. Then a slow, hot, salmon-coloured flush stole over his face, and he turned abruptly round.

The Needle's Eye was a hole in the ancient grey rock, like a window, looking to England; England at the moment in shadow. A stream wound and glinted in the flat shadow, and beyond that the flat, insignificant hills heaped in mounds of shade. Cloud was coming--the English side was in shadow. Wales was still in the sun, but the shadow was spreading. The day was going to disappoint them. Lou was a tiny bit chilled already.

Luncheon was still several miles away. The party hastened down to the horses. Lou picked a few sprigs of ling, and some harebells, and some straggling yellow flowers: not because she wanted them, but to distract herself. The atmosphere of 'enjoying ourselves' was becoming cruel to her: it sapped all the life out of her. "Oh, if only I needn't enjoy myself," she moaned inwardly. But the Manby girls were enjoying themselves so much. "I think it's frantically lovely up here," said the other one--not Flora--Elsie.

"It is beautiful, isn't it! I'm so glad you like it," replied Rico. And he was really relieved and gratified, because the other one said she was enjoying it so frightfully. He dared not say to Lou, as he wanted to: "I'm afraid, Lou, darling, you don't love it as much as we do."--He was afraid of her answer: "No, dear, I don't love it at all! I want to be away from these people."

Slightly piqued, he rode on with the Manby group, and Lou came behind with her mother. Cloud was covering the sky with grey. There was a cold wind. Everybody was anxious to get to the farm for luncheon, and be safely home before rain came.

They were riding along one of the narrow little foot-tracks, mere grooves of grass between heather and bright green bilberry. The blond young man was ahead, then his wife, then Flora, then Rico. Lou, from a little distance, watched the glossy, powerful haunches of St. Mawr swaying with life, always too much life, like a menace. The fair young man was whistling a new dance tune.

"That's an awfully attractive tune," Rico called. "Do whistle it again, Fred, I should like to memorise it."

Fred began to whistle it again.

At that moment St. Mawr exploded again, shied sideways as if a bomb had gone off, and kept backing through the heather.

"Fool!" cried Rico, thoroughly unnerved: he had been terribly sideways in the saddle, Lou had feared he was going to fall. But he got his seat, and pulled the reins viciously, to bring the horse to order, and put him on the track again. St. Mawr began to rear: his favourite trick. Rico got him forward a few yards, when up he went again.

"Fool!" yelled Rico, hanging in the air.

He pulled the horse over backwards on top of him.

Lou gave a loud, unnatural, horrible scream: she heard it herself, at the same time as she heard the crash of the falling horse. Then she saw a pale gold belly, and hoofs that worked and flashed in the air, and St. Mawr writhing, straining his head terrifically upwards, his great eyes starting from the naked lines of his nose. With a great neck arching cruelly from the ground, he was pulling frantically at the reins, which Rico still held tight.--Yes, Rico, lying strangely sideways, his eyes also starting from his yellow-white face, among the heather, still clutched the reins.

Young Edwards was rushing forward, and circling round the writhing, immense horse, whose pale-gold, inverted bulk seemed to fill the universe.

"Let him get up, Carrington! Let him get up!" he was yelling, darting warily near to get the reins.--Another spasmodic convulsion of the horse.

Horror! The young man reeled backwards with his face in his hands. He had got a kick in the race. Red blood running down his chin!

Lewis was there, on the ground, getting the reins out of Rico's hands. St. Mawr gave a great curve like a fish, spread his forefeet on the earth and reared his head, looking round in a ghastly fashion. His eyes were arched, his nostrils wide, his face ghastly in a sort of panic. He rested thus, seated with his forefeet planted and his face in panic, almost like some terrible lizard, for several moments. Then he heaved sickeningly to his feet, and stood convulsed, trembling.

There lay Rico, crumpled and rather sideways, staring at the heavens from a yellow, dead-looking face. Lewis, glancing round in a sort of horror, looked in dread at St. Mawr again. Flora had been hovering.--She now rushed screeching to the prostrate Rico:

"Harry! Harry! you're not dead! Oh, Harry! Harry! Harry!"

Lou had dismounted.--She didn't know when. She stood a little way off, as if spellbound, while Flora cried: *Harry! Harry! Harry!*

Suddenly Rico sat up.

"Where is the horse?" he said.

At the same time an added whiteness came on his face, and he bit his lip with pain, and he fell prostrate again in a faint. Flora rushed to put her arm round him.

Where was the horse? He had backed slowly away, in an agony of suspicion, while Lewis murmured to him in vain. His head was raised again, the eyes still starting from their sockets, and a terrible guilty, ghost-like look on his face. When Lewis drew a little nearer he twitched and shrank like a shaken steel spring, away-

-not to be touched. He seemed to be seeing legions of ghosts, down the dark avenues of all the centuries that have lapsed since the horse became subject to man.

And the other young man? He was still standing, at a little distance, with his face in his hands, motionless, the blood falling on his white shirt, and his wife at his side, pleading, distracted.

Mrs. Witt, too, was there, as if cast in steel, watching. She made no sound and did not move, only from a fixed, impassive face, watched each thing.

"Do tell me what you think is the matter," Lou pleaded, distracted, to Flora, who was supporting Rico and weeping torrents of unknown tears.

Then Mrs. Witt came forward and began in a very practical manner to unclose the shirt-neck and feel the young man's heart. Rico opened his eyes again, said *"Really!"* and closed his eyes once more.

"It's fainting!" said Mrs. Witt. "We have no brandy." Lou, too weary to be able to feel anything, said:

"I'll go and get some."

She went to her alarmed horse, who stood among the others with her head down, in suspense. Almost unconsciously Lou mounted, set her face ahead, and was riding away.

Then Poppy shied too, with a sudden start, and Lou pulled up. "Why?" she said to her horse. "Why did you do that?"

She looked round, and saw in the heather a glimpse of yellow and black.

"A snake!" she said wonderingly.

And she looked closer.

It was a dead adder that had been drinking at a reedy pool in a little depression just off the road, and had been killed with stones. There it lay, also crumpled, its head crushed, its gold-and-yellow back still glittering dully, and a bit of pale-blue showing, killed that morning.

Lou rode on, her face set towards the farm. An unspeakable weariness had overcome her. She .could not even suffer. Weariness of spirit left her in a sort of apathy.

And she had a vision, a vision of evil. Or not strictly a vision. She became aware of evil, evil, evil, rolling in great waves over the earth. Always she had thought there was-no such thing--only a mere negation of good. Now, like an ocean to whose surface she had risen, she saw the dark-grey waves of evil rearing in a great tide.

And it had swept mankind away without mankind's knowing. It had caught up the nations as the rising ocean might lift the fishes, and was sweeping them on in a great tide of evil. They did not know. The people did not know. They did not even wish it. They wanted to be good and to have everything joyful and enjoyable. Everything joyful and enjoyable: for everybody. This was what they wanted, if you asked them.

But at the same time, they had fallen under the spell of evil. It was a soft, subtle thing, soft as water, and its motion was soft and imperceptible, as the running of a tide is invisible to one who is out on the ocean. And they were all out on the ocean, being borne along in the current of the mysterious evil, creatures of the evil principle, as fishes are creatures of the sea.

There was no relief. The whole world was enveloped in one great flood. All the nations, the white, the brown, the black, the yellow, all were immersed, in the strange tide of evil that was subtly, irresistibly rising. No one, perhaps, deliberately wished it. Nearly every individual wanted peace and a good time all round: everybody to have a good time.

But some strange thing had happened, and the vast mysterious force of positive evil was let loose. She felt that from the core of Asia the evil welled up, as from some strange pole, and slowly was drowning earth.

It was something horrifying, something you could not escape from. It had come to her as in a vision, when she saw the pale gold belly of the stallion upturned, the hoofs working wildly, the wicked curved hams of the horse, and then the evil straining of that arched, fish-like neck, with the dilated eyes of the head. Thrown backwards, and working its hoofs in the air. Reversed, and purely evil.

She saw the same in people. They were thrown backwards, and writhing with evil. And the rider, crushed, was still reining them down.

What did it mean? Evil, evil, and a rapid return to the sordid chaos. Which was wrong, the horse or the rider? Or both?

She thought with horror of St. Mawr, and of the look on his face. But she thought with horror, a colder horror, of Rico's face as he snarled *Fool!* His fear, his impotence as a master, as a rider, his presumption. And she thought with horror of those other people, so glib, so glibly evil.

What did they want to do, those Manby girls? Undermine, undermine, undermine. They wanted to undermine Rico, just as that fair young man would have liked to undermine her. Believe in nothing, care about nothing: but keep the surface easy, and have a good time. *Let us undermine one another. There is nothing to believe in, so let us undermine everything. But look out! No scenes, no spoiling the game. Stick to the rules of the game. Be sporting, and don't do anything that would make a commotion. Keep the game going smooth and jolly, and bear your bit like a sport. Never, by any chance, injure your fellow-man openly. But always injure him secretly. Make a fool of him, and undermine his nature. Break him up by undermining him, if you can. It's good sport.*

The evil! The mysterious potency of evil. She could see it all the time, in individuals, in society, in the press. There it was in socialism and bolshevism: the same evil. But bolshevism made a mess of the outside of life, so turn it down. Try fascism. Fascism would keep the surface of life intact, and carry on the undermining business all the better. All the better sport. Never draw blood. Keep the hemorrhage internal, invisible.

And as soon as fascism makes a break--which it is bound to, because all evil works up to a break--then turn it down. With gusto, turn it down.

Mankind, like a horse, ridden by a stranger, smooth-faced, evil rider. Evil himself, smooth-faced and pseudo-handsome, riding mankind past the dead snake, to the last break.

Mankind no longer its own master. Ridden by this pseudo-handsome ghoul of outward loyalty, inward treachery, in a game of betrayal, betrayal, betrayal. The last of the gods of our era, Judas supreme!

People performing outward acts of loyalty, piety, self-sacrifice. But inwardly bent on undermining, betraying. Directing all their subtle evil will against any positive living thing. Masquerading as the ideal, in order to poison the real.

Creation destroys as it goes, throws down one tree for the rise of another. But ideal mankind would abolish death, multiply itself million upon million, rear up city upon city, save every parasite alive, until the accumulation of mere existence is swollen to a horror. But go on saving life, the ghastly salvation army of ideal mankind. At the same time secretly, viciously, potently undermine the natural creation, betray it with kiss after kiss, destroy it from the inside, till you have the swollen rottenness of our teeming existences.--But keep the game going. Nobody's going to make another bad break, such as Germany and Russia made.

Two bad breaks the secret evil has made: in Germany and in Russia. Watch it! Let evil keep a policeman's eye on evil! The surface of life must remain unruptured. Production must be heaped upon production. And the natural creation must be betrayed by many more kisses, yet. Judas is the last God, and, by heaven, the most potent.

But even Judas made a break: hanged himself, and his bowels gushed out. Not long after his triumph.

Man must destroy as he goes, as trees fall for trees to rise. The accumulation of life and things means rottenness. Life must destroy life, in the unfolding of creation. We save up life at the expense of the unfolding, till all is full of rottenness. Then at last we make a break.

What's to be done? Generally speaking, nothing. The dead will have to bury their dead, while the earth stinks of corpses. The individual can but depart from the mass, and try to cleanse himself. Try to hold fast to the living thing, which destroys as it goes, but remains sweet. And in his soul fight, fight, fight to preserve that which is life in him from the ghastly kisses and poison-bites of the myriad evil ones. Retreat to the desert, and fight. But in his soul adhere to that which is life itself, creatively destroying as it goes: destroying the stiff old thing to let the new bud come through. The one passionate principle of creative being, which recognises the natural good, and has a sword for the swarms of evil. Fights, fights, fights to protect itself. But with itself, is strong and at peace.

Lou came to the farm, and got brandy, and asked the men to come out to carry in the injured.

It turned out that the kick in the face had knocked a couple of young Edwards's teeth out, and would disfigure him a little.

"To go through the war, and then get this!" he mumbled, with a vindictive glance at St. Mawr.

And it turned out that Rico had two broken ribs and a crushed ankle. Poor Rico, he would limp for life.

"I want St. Mawr *shot!*" was almost his first word when he was in bed at the farm and Lou was sitting beside him. "What good would that do, dear?" she said.

"The brute is evil. I want him *shot!*"

Rico could make the last word sound like the spitting of a bullet.

"Do you want to shoot him yourself?"

"No. But I want to have him shot. I shall never be easy till I know he has a bullet through him. He's got a wicked character. I don't feel you are safe with him down there. I shall get one of the Manbys' gamekeepers to shoot him. You might tell Flora--or I'll tell her myself, when she comes."

"Don't talk about it now, dear. You've got a temperature."

Was it true St. Mawr was evil? She would never forget him writhing and lunging on the ground, nor his awful face when he reared up. But then that noble look of his: surely he was not mean? Whereas all evil had an inner meanness, mean! Was he mean? Was he meanly treacherous? Did he know he could kill, and meanly wait his opportunity?

She was afraid. And if this were true, then he *should* be shot. Perhaps he ought to be shot.

This thought haunted her. Was there something mean and treacherous in St. Mawr's spirit, the vulgar evil? If so, then have him shot. At moments, an anger would rise in her, as she thought of his frenzied rearing, and his mad, hideous writhing on the ground, and in the heat of her anger she would want to hurry down to her mother's house and have the creature shot at once. It would be a satisfaction, and a vindication of human rights. Because after all, Rico was so considerate of the brutal horse. But not a spark of consideration did the stallion have for Rico. No, it was the slavish malevolence of a domesticated creature that kept cropping up in St. Mawr. The slave, taking his slavish vengeance, then dropping back into subservience.

All the slaves of this world, accumulating their preparations for slavish vengeance, and then, when they have taken it, ready to drop back into servility. Freedom! Most slaves can't be freed, no matter how you let them loose. Like domestic animals, they are, in the long run, more afraid of freedom than of masters: and freed by some generous master, they will at last crawl back to some mean boss, who will have no scruples about kicking them. Because, for them, far better kicks and servility than the hard, lonely responsibility of real freedom.

The wild animal is at every moment intensely self-disciplined, poised in the tension of self-defence, self-preservation and self-assertion. The moments of relaxation are rare and most carefully chosen. Even sleep is watchful, guarded, unrelaxing, the wild courage pitched one degree higher than the wild fear. Courage, the wild thing's courage to maintain itself alone and living in the midst of a diverse universe.

Did St. Mawr have this courage?

And did Rico?

Ah, Rico! He was one of mankind's myriad conspirators, who conspire to live in absolute physical safety, whilst willing the minor disintegration of all positive living.

But St. Mawr? Was it the natural wild thing in him which caused these disasters? Or was it the slave, asserting himself for vengeance?

If the latter, let him be shot. It would be a great satisfaction to see him dead.

But if the former--

When she could leave Rico with the nurse, she motored down to her mother for a couple of days. Rico lay in bed at the farm.

Everything seemed curiously changed. There was a new silence about the place, a new coolness. Summer had passed with several thunderstorms, and the blue, cool touch of autumn was about the house. Dahlias and perennial yellow sunflowers were out, the yellow of ending summer, the red coals of early autumn. First mauve tips of Michaelmas daisies were showing. Something suddenly carried her away to the great bare spaces of Texas, the blue sky, the flat, burnt earth, the miles of sunflowers. Another sky, another silence, towards the setting sun.

And suddenly she craved again for the more absolute silence of America. English stillness was so soft, like an inaudible murmur of voices, of presences. But the silence in the empty spaces of America was still unutterable, almost cruel.

St. Mawr was in a small field by himself: she could not bear that he should be always in stable. Slowly she went through the gate towards him. And he stood there looking at her, the bright bay creature.

She could tell he was feeling somewhat subdued, after his late escapade. He was aware of the general human condemnation: the human damning. But something obstinate and uncanny in him made him not relent.

"Hello! St. Mawr!" she said, as she drew near, and he stood watching her, his ears pricked, his big eyes glancing sideways at her.

But he moved away when she wanted to touch him. "Don't trouble," she said. "I don't want to catch you or do anything to you."

He stood still, listening to the sound of her voice, and giving quick, small glances at her. His underlip trembled. But he did not blink. His eyes remained wide and unrelenting. There was a curious malicious obstinacy in him which roused her anger.

"I don't want to touch you," she said. "I only want to look at you, and even you can't prevent that."

She stood gazing hard at him, wanting to know, to settle the question of his meanness or his spirit. A thing with a brave spirit is not mean.

He was uneasy as she watched him. He pretended to hear something, the mares two fields away, and he lifted his head and neighed. She knew the powerful, splendid sound so well: like bells made of living membrane. And he looked so noble again, with his head tilted up, listening, and his male eyes looking proudly over the distance, eagerly.

But it was all a bluff.

He knew, and became silent again. And as he stood there a few yards away from her, his head lifted and wary, his body full of power and tension, his face slightly averted from her, she felt a great animal sadness come from him. A strange animal atmosphere of sadness, that was vague and disseminated through the air, and made her feel as though she breathed grief. She breathed it into her breast, as if it were a great sigh down the ages, that passed into her breast. And she felt a great woe: the woe of human unworthiness. The race of men judged in the consciousness of the animals they have subdued, and there found unworthy, ignoble.

Ignoble men, unworthy of the animals they have subjugated, bred the woe in the spirit of their creatures. St. Mawr, that bright horse, one of the kings of creation in the order below man, it had been a fulfilment for him to serve the brave, reckless, perhaps cruel men of the past, who had a flickering, rising flame of nobility in them. To serve that flame of mysterious further nobility. Nothing matters, but that strange flame, of inborn nobility that obliges men to be brave, and onward plunging. And the horse will bear him on.

But now where is the flame of dangerous, forward-pressing nobility in men? Dead, dead, guttering out in a stink of self-sacrifice whose feeble light is a light of exhaustion and *laissez-faire*.

And the horse, is he to go on carrying man forward into this?--this gutter?

No! Man wisely invents motor-cars and other machines, automobile and locomotive. The horse is superannuated for man.

But alas, man is even more superannuated for the horse.

Dimly in a woman's muse, Lou realised this, as she breathed the horse's sadness, his accumulated vague woe from the generations of latter-day ignobility. And a grief and a sympathy flooded her, for the horse. She realised now how his sadness recoiled into these frenzies of obstinacy and malevolence. Underneath it all was grief, an unconscious, vague, pervading animal grief, which perhaps only Lewis understood, because he felt the same. The grief of the generous creature which sees all ends turning to the morass of ignoble living.

She did not want to say any more to the horse: she did not want to look at him any more. The grief flooded her soul, that made her want to be alone. She knew now what it all amounted to. She knew that the horse, born to serve nobly, had waited in vain for someone noble to serve. His spirit knew that nobility had gone out of men. And this left him high and dry, in a sort of despair.

As she walked away from him, towards the gate, slowly he began to walk after her.

Phoenix came striding through the gate towards her.

"You not afraid of that horse?" he asked sardonically, in his quiet, subtle voice.

"Not at the present moment," she replied, even more quietly, looking direct at him. She was not in any mood to be jeered at.

And instantly the sardonic grimace left his face, followed by the sudden blankness, and the look of race misery in the keen eyes.

"Do you want me to be afraid?" she said, continuing to the gate.

"No, I don't want it," he replied, dejected.

"Are you afraid of him yourself?" she said, glancing round. St. Mawr had stopped, seeing Phoenix, and had turned away again.

"I'm not afraid of no horses," said Phoenix.

Lou went on quietly. At the gate, she asked him: "Don't you like St. Mawr, Phoenix?"

"I like him. He's a very good horse."

"Even after what he's done to Sir Henry?"

"That don't make no difference to him being a good horse."

"But suppose he'd done it to you?"

"I don't care. I say it my own fault."

"Don't you think he is wicked?"

"I don't think so. He don't kick anybody. He don't bite anybody. He don't pitch, he don't buck, he don't do nothing."

"He rears," said Lou.

"Well, what is rearing?" said the man, with a slow, contemptuous smile.

"A good deal, when a horse falls back on you."

"That horse don't want to fall back on you, if you don't make him. If you know how to ride him. That horse wants his own way some time. If you don't let him, you got to fight him. Then look out!"

"Look out he doesn't kill you, you mean!"

"Look out you don't let him," said Phoenix, with his slow, grim, sardonic smile.

Lou watched the smooth, golden face with its thin line of moustache and its sad eyes with the glint in them. Cruel--there was something cruel in him, right down in the abyss of him. But at the same time, there was an aloneness, and a grim little satisfaction in a fight, and the peculiar courage of an inherited despair. People who inherit despair may at last turn it into greater heroism. It was almost so with Phoenix. Three-quarters of his blood was probably Indian and the remaining quarter, that came through the Mexican father, had the Spanish-American despair to add to the Indian. It was almost complete enough to leave him free to be heroic.

"What are we going to do with him, though?" she asked. "Why don't you and Mrs. Witt go back to America--you never been West. You go West."

"Where, to California?"

"No. To Arizona or New Mexico or Colorado or Wyoming, anywhere. Not to California."

Phoenix looked at her keenly, and she saw the desire dark in him. He wanted to go back. But he was afraid to go back alone, empty-handed, as it were. He had suffered too much, and in that country his sufferings would overcome him, unless he had some other background. He had been too much in contact with the white world, and his own world was too dejected, in a sense, too hopeless for his own hopelessness. He needed an alien contact to give him relief.

But he wanted to go back. His necessity to go back was becoming too strong for him.

"What is it like in Arizona?" she asked. "Isn't it all pale-coloured sand and alkali, and a few cactuses, and terribly hot and deathly?"

"No!" he cried. "I don't take you there. I take you to the mountains--trees--" he lifted up his hand and looked at the sky--"big trees--pine! *Pino-real* and *pinovetes*, smell good. And then you come down, *piñon*, not very tall, and cedro, cedar, smell good in the fire. And then you see the desert, away below, go miles and miles, and where the canyon go, the crack where it look red! I know, I been there, working a cattle ranch."

He looked at her with a haunted glow in his dark eyes. The poor fellow was suffering from nostalgia. And as he glowed at her in that queer, mystical way, she too seemed to see that country, with its dark, heavy mountains holding in their lap the great stretches of pale, creased, silent desert that still is virgin of idea, its word unspoken.

Phoenix was watching her closely and subtly. He wanted something of her. He wanted it intensely, heavily, and he watched her as if he could force her to give it him. He wanted her to take him back to America, because, rudderless, he was afraid to go back alone. He wanted her to take him back: avidly he wanted it. She was to be the means to his end.

Why shouldn't he go back by himself? Why should he crave for her to go too? Why should he want her there?

There was no answer, except that he did.

"Why, Phoenix," she said, "I might possibly go back to America. But you know, Sir Henry would never go there. He doesn't like America, though he's never been. But I'm sure he'd never go there to live."

"Let him stay here," said Phoenix abruptly, the sardonic look on his face as he watched her face. "You come, and let him stay here."

"Ah, that's a whole story!" she said, and moved away.

As she went, he looked after her, standing silent and arrested and watching as an Indian watches. It was not love. Personal love counts so little when the greater griefs, the greater hopes, the great despairs and the great resolutions come upon us.

She found Mrs. Witt rather more silent, more firmly closed within herself, than usual. Her mouth was shut tight, her brows were arched rather more imperiously than ever, she was revolving some inward problem about which Lou was far too wise to inquire.

In the afternoon Dean Vyner and Mrs. Vyner came to call on Lady Carrington.

"What bad luck this is, Lady Carrington!" said the Dean. "Knocks Scotland on the head for you this year, I'm afraid. How did you leave your husband?"

"He seems to be doing as well as he could dot" said Lou. "But how very unfortunate!" murmured the invalid Mrs. Vyner. "Such a handsome young man, in the bloom of youth! Does he suffer much pain?"

"Chiefly his foot," said Lou.

"Oh, I do so hope they'll be able to restore the ankle. Oh, how dreadful, to be lamed at his age!"

"The doctor doesn't know. There may be a limp," said Lou.

"That horse has certainly left his mark on two good-looking young fellows," said the Dean. "If you don't mind my saying so, Lady Carrington, I think he's a bad egg."

"Who, St. Mawr?" said Lou, in her American sing-song.

"Yes, Lady Carrington," murmured Mrs. Vyner, in her invalid's low tone. "Don't you think he ought to be put away? He seems to me the incarnation of cruelty. His neigh. It goes through me like knives. Cruel! Cruel! Oh, I think he should be put away."

"How put away?" murmured Lou, taking on an invalid's low tone herself.

"Shot, I suppose," said the Dean.

"It is quite painless. He'll know nothing," murmured Mrs. Vyner hastily. "And think of the harm he has done already! Horrible! Horrible!" she shuddered. "Poor Sir Henry lame for life, and Freddy Edwards disfigured. Besides all that has gone before. Ah, no, such a creature ought not to live!";

"To live, and have a groom to look after him and feed him," said the Dean. "It's a bit thick, while he's smashing up the very people that give him bread--or oats, since he's a horse. But I suppose you'll be wanting to get rid of him?"

"Rico does," murmured Lou.

"Very naturally. So should I. A vicious horse is worse than a vicious man-- except that you are free to put him six feet underground, and end his vice finally, by your own act."

"Do you think St. Mawr is vicious?" said Lou.

"Well, of course--if we're driven to definitions!--I *know* he's dangerous."

"And do you think we ought to shoot everything that is dangerous?" asked Lou, her colour rising.

"But, Lady Carrington, have you consulted your husband? Surely his wish should be law, in a matter of this sort? And on such an occasion! For you, who are a woman, it is enough that the horse is cruel, cruel, evil! I felt it long before anything happened. That evil male cruelty! Ah!" and she clasped her hands convulsively.

"I suppose," said Lou slowly, "that St. Mawr is really Rico's horse: I gave him to him, I suppose. But I don't believe I could let him shoot him, for all that."

"Ah, Lady Carrington," said the Dean breezily, "you can shift the responsibility. The horse is a public menace, put it at that. We can get an order to have him done away with, at the public expense. And among ourselves we can find some suitable compensation for you, as a mark of sympathy. Which, believe me, is very sincere! One hates to have to destroy a fine-looking animal. But I would sacrifice a dozen rather than have our Rico limping."

"Yes, indeed," murmured Mrs. Vyner.

"Will you excuse me one moment, while I see about tea," said Lou, rising and leaving the room. Her colour was high, and there was a glint in her eyes. These people almost roused her to hatred. Oh, these awful, house-bred, house-inbred human beings, how repulsive they were!

She hurried to her mother's dressing-room. Mrs. Witt was very carefully putting a touch of red on her lips.

"Mother, they want to shoot St. Mawr," she said.

"I know," said Mrs. Witt, as calmly as if Lou had said tea was ready.

"Well--" stammered Lou, rather put out. "Don't you think it cheek?"

"It depends, I suppose, on the point of view," said Mrs. Witt dispassionately, looking closely at her lips. "I don't think the English climate agrees with me. I need something to stand up against, no matter whether it's great heat or great cold. This climate, like the food and the people, is most always lukewarm or tepid, one or the other. And the tepid and the lukewarm are not really my line." She spoke with a slow drawl.

"But they're in the drawing-room, mother, trying to force me to have St. Mawr killed."

"What about tea?" said Mrs. Witt.

"I don't care," said Lou.

Mrs. Witt worked the bell-handle.

"I suppose, Louise," she said, in her most beaming eighteenth-century manner, "that these are your guests, so you will preside over the ceremony of pouring out."

"No, mother, you do it. I can't smile to-day."

"I can," said Mrs. Witt.

And she bowed her head slowly, with a faint, ceremoniously-effusive smile, as if handing a cup of tea. Lou's face flickered to a smile.

"Then you pour out for them. You can stand them better than I can."

"Yes," said Mrs. Witt. "I saw Mrs. Vyner's hat coming across the churchyard. It looks so like a crumpled cup and saucer, that I have been saying to myself ever since: 'Dear Mrs. Vyner, can't I fill your cup!'--and then pouring tea into that hat. And I hear the Dean responding: 'My head is covered with cream, my cup runneth over.'--That is the way they make me feel."

They marched downstairs, and Mrs. Witt poured tea with that devastating correctness which made Mrs. Vyner, who was utterly impervious to sarcasm, pronounce her 'indecipherably vulgar'.

But the Dean was the old bull-dog, and he had set his teeth in a subject.

"I was talking to Lady Carrington about that stallion, Mrs. Witt."

"Did you say stallion?" asked Mrs. Witt, with perfect neutrality.

"Why, yes, I presume that's what he is."

"I presume so," said Mrs. Witt colourlessly.

"I'm afraid Lady Carrington is a little sensitive on the wrong score," said the Dean.

"I beg your pardon," said Mrs. Witt, leaning forward in her most colourless polite manner. "You mean the stallion's score?"

"Yes," said the Dean testily. "The horse St. Mawr."

"The stallion St. Mawr," echoed Mrs. Witt, with utmost mild vagueness. She completely ignored Mrs. Vyner, who felt plunged like a specimen into methylated spirit. There was a moment's full-stop.

"Yes?" said Mrs. Witt naively.

"You agree that we can't have any more of these accidents to your young men?" said the Dean rather hastily.

"I certainly do!" Mrs. Witt spoke very slowly, and the Dean's lady began to look up. She might find a loop-hole through which to wriggle into the contest. "You know, Dean, that my son-in-law calls me, for preference, *belle-mère*! It sounds so awfully English when he says it: I always see myself as an old grey mare with a bell round her neck, leading a bunch of horses." She smiled a prim little smile, very conversationally. "Well!" and she pulled herself up from the aside. "Now as the bell-mare of the bunch of horses, I shall see to it that my son-in-law doesn't go too near that stallion again. That stallion won't stand mischief."

She spoke so earnestly that the Dean looked at her with round, wide eyes, completely taken aback.

"We all know, Mrs. Witt, that the author of the mischief is St. Mawr himself," he said, in a loud tone.

"Really! you think *that*?" Her voice went up in American surprise. "Why, how *strange--!"* and she lingered over the last word.

"Strange, eh?--After what's just happened?" said the Dean, with a deadly little smile.

"Why, yes! Most strange! I saw with my own eyes my son-in-law pull that stallion over backwards, and hold him down with the reins as tight as he could hold them; pull St. Mawr's head backwards on to the ground, till the groom had to crawl up and force the reins out of my son-in-law's hands. Don't you think that was mischievous on Sir Henry's part?"

The Dean was growing purple. He made an apoplectic movement with his hand. Mrs. Vyner was turned to a seated pillar of salt, strangely dressed up.

"Mrs. Witt, you are playing on words."

"No, Dean Vyner, I am not. My son-in-law pulled that horse over backwards and pinned him down with the reins."

"I am sorry for the horse," said the Dean, with heavy sarcasm.

"I am *very*," said Mrs. Witt, "sorry for that stallion: *very!*" Here Mrs. Vyner rose as if a chair-spring had suddenly pro-pelled her to her feet. She was streaky pink in the face.

"Mrs. Witt," she panted, "you misdirect your sympathies. That poor young man--in the beauty of youth."

"Isn't he *beautiful*--" murmured Mrs. Witt, extravagantly in sympathy. "He's my daughter's husband!" And she looked at the petrified Lou.

"Certainly!" panted the Dean's wife. "And you can defend that--that--"

"That stallion," said Mrs. Witt. "But you see, Mrs. Vyner," she added, leaning forward female and confidential, "if the old grey mare doesn't defend the stallion, who will? All the blooming young ladies will defend my beautiful son-in-law. You feel so *warmly* for him yourself! I'm an American woman, and I always have to stand up for the accused. And I stand up for that stallion. I say it is not right. He was pulled over backwards and then pinned down by my son-in-law--who may have meant to do it, or may not. And now people abuse him.--Just tell everybody, Mrs. Vyner and Dean Vyner"--she looked round at the Dean--"that the *belle-mère's* sympathies are with the stallion."

She looked from one to the other with a faint and gracious little bow, her black eyebrows arching in her eighteenth-century face like black rainbows, and her full, bold, grey eyes absolutely incomprehensible.

"Well, it's a peculiar message to have to hand round, Mrs. Witt," the Dean began to boom, when she interrupted him by laying her hand on his arm and leaning forward, looking up into his face like a clinging, pleading female:

"Oh, but *do* hand it, Dean, do hand it," she pleaded, gazing intently into his face.

He backed uncomfortably from that gaze.

"Since you wish it," he said, in a chest voice.

"I most certainly do--" she said, as if she were wishing the sweetest wish on earth. Then turning to Mrs. Vyner:

"Good-bye, Mrs. Vyner. We *do* appreciate your coming, my daughter and I."

"I came out of kindness----" said Mrs. Vyner.

"Oh, I know it, I know it," said Mrs. Witt. "Thank you so much. Good-bye! Good-bye, Dean! Who is taking the morning service on Sunday? I hope it is you, because I want to come."

"It is me," said the Dean. "Good-bye! Well, good-bye, Lady Carrington. I shall be going over to see our young man to-morrow, and will gladly take you or anything you have to send."

"Perhaps mother would like to go," said Lou softly, plaintively.

"Well, we shall see," said the Dean. "Good-bye for the present!"

Mother and daughter stood at the window watching the two cross the churchyard. Dean and wife knew it, but daren't look round, and daren't admit the fact to one another.

Lou was grinning with a complete grin that gave her an odd, dryad or faun look, intensified.

"It was almost as good as pouring tea into her hat," said Mrs. Witt serenely. "People like that tire me out. I shall take a glass of sherry."

"So will I, mother.--It was even better than pouring tea in her hat.--You meant, didn't you, if you poured tea in her hat, to put cream and sugar in first?"

"I did," said Mrs. Witt.

But after the excitement of the encounter had passed away, Lou felt as if her life had passed away too. She went to bed, feeling she could stand no more.

In the morning she found her mother sitting at a window watching a funeral. It was raining heavily, so that some of the mourners even wore mackintosh coats. The funeral was in the poorer corner of the churchyard, where another new grave was covered with wreaths of sodden, shrivelling flowers. The yellowish coffin stood on wet earth in the rain: the curate held his hat, in a sort of permanent salute, above his head, like a little umbrella, as he hastened on with the service. The people seemed too wet to weep more wet.

It was a long coffin.

"Mother, do you really *like* watching?" asked Lou irritably, as Mrs. Witt sat in complete absorption.

"I do, Louise, I really enjoy it."

"Enjoy, mother!"--Lou was almost disgusted.

"I'll tell you why. I imagine I'm the one in the coffin--this is a girl of eighteen, who died of consumption--and those are my relatives, and I'm watching them put me away. And, you know, Louise, I've come to the conclusion that hardly anybody in the world really lives, and so hardly anybody really dies. They may well say: 'Oh, Death, where is thy sting-a-ling-a-ling?' Even Death can't sting those that have never really lived.--I always used to want that--to die without death stinging me.--And I'm sure the girl in the coffin is saying to herself: 'Fancy Aunt Emma putting on a drab slicker, and wearing it while they bury me. Doesn't show much respect. But then my mother's family always were common!' I feel there should be a solemn burial of a roll of newspapers containing the account of the death and funeral next week. It would be just as serious: the grave of all the world's remarks--"

"I don't want to think about it, mother. One ought to be able to laugh at it. I want to laugh at it."

"Well, Louise, I think it's just as great a mistake to laugh at everything as to cry at everything. Laughter's not the one panacea, either. I should *really* like, before I do come to be buried in a box, to know where I am. That young girl in that coffin never was anywhere--any more than the newspaper remarks on her death and burial. And I begin to wonder if I've ever been anywhere. I seem to have been a daily sequence of newspaper remarks myself. I'm sure I never really conceived you and gave you birth. It all happened in newspaper notices. It's a newspaper fact that you are my child, and that's about all there is to it."

Lou smiled as she listened.

"I always knew you were philosophic, mother. But I never dreamed at would come to elegies in a country churchyard, written to your motherhood."

"Exactly, Louise! Here I sit and sing the elegy to my own motherhood. I never had any motherhood, except in newspaper fact. I never was a wife, except in newspaper notices. I never was a young girl, except in newspaper remarks. Bury everything I ever said or that was said about me, and you've buried *me*. But since Kind Words Can Never Die, I can't be buried, and death has no sting-a-ling-a-ling for *me*!--Now listen to me, Louise: I want death to be real to me--not as it was to that young girl. I *want* it to hurt me, Louise. If it hurts me enough, I shall know I was alive."

She set her face and gazed under half-dropped lids at the funeral, stoic, fate-like, and yet, for the first time, with a certain pure wistfulness of a young, virgin girl. This frightened Lou very much. She was so used to the matchless Amazon in her mother, that when she saw her sit there, still, wistful, virginal, tender as a girl who has never taken armour, wistful at the window that only looked on graves, a serious terror took hold of the young woman. The terror of too late!

Lou felt years, centuries older than her mother at that moment, with the tiresome responsibility of youth to protect and guide their elders.

"What can we do about it, mother?" she asked protectively.

"Do nothing, Louise. I'm not going to have anybody wisely steering my canoe, now I feel the rapids are near. I shall go with the river. Don't you pretend to do anything for me. I've done enough mischief myself, that way. I'm going down the stream at last."

There was a pause.

"But in actuality, what?" asked Lou, a little ironically. "I don't quite know. Wait a while."

"Go back to America?"

"That is possible."

"I may come too."

"I've always waited for you to go back of your own will."

Lou went away, wandering round the house. She was so unutterably tired of everything--weary of the house, the graveyard, weary of the thought of Rico. She would have to go back to him to-morrow, to nurse him. Poor old Rico, going on like an amiable machine from day to day. It wasn't his fault. But his life was a rattling nullity, and her life rattled in null correspondence. She had hardly strength enough to stop rattling and be still. Perhaps she had not strength enough.

She did not know. She felt so weak that unless something carried her away she would go on rattling her bit in the great machine of human life till she collapsed and her rattle rattled itself out, and there was a sort of barren silence where the sound of her had been.

She wandered out in the rain to the coach-house, where Lewis and Phoenix were sitting facing one another, one on a bin, the other on the inner doorstep.

"Well," she said, smiling oddly. "What's to be done?"

The two men stood up. Outside the rain fell steadily on the flagstones of the yard, past the leaves of trees. Lou sat down on the little iron step of the dog-cart.

"That's cold," said Phoenix. "You sit here." And he threw a yellow horse-blanket on the box where he had been sitting. "I don't want to take your seat," she said.

"All right, you take it."

He moved across and sat gingerly on the shaft of the dogcart. Lou seated herself and loosened her soft tartan shawl. Her face was pink and fresh, and her dark hair curled almost merrily in the damp. But under her eyes were the finger-prints of deadly weariness.

She looked up at the two men, again smiling in her odd fashion.

"What are we going to do?" she asked.

They looked at her closely, seeking her meaning.

"What about?" said Phoenix, a faint smile reflecting on his face, merely because she smiled.

"Oh, everything," she said, hugging her shawl again. "You know what they want? They want to shoot St. Mawr." The two men exchanged glances.

"Who want it?" said Phoenix.

"Why--all our *friends!*" She made a little *moue.* "Dean Vyner does."

Again the men exchanged glances. There was a pause. Then Phoenix said, looking aside:

"The boss is selling him."

"Who?"

"Sir Henry."--The half-breed always spoke the title with difficulty, and with a sort of sneer. "He sell him to Miss Manby."

"How do you know?"

"The man from Corrabach told me last night. Flora, she say it."

Lou's eyes met the sardonic, empty-seeing eyes of Phoenix direct. There was too much sarcastic understanding. She looked aside.

"What else did he say?" she asked.

"I don't know," said Phoenix evasively. "He say they cut him--else shoot him. Think they cut him--and if he die, he die."

Lou understood. He meant they would geld St. Mawr--at his age.

She looked at Lewis. He sat with his head down, so she could not see his face.

"Do you think it is true?" she asked. "Lewis? Do you think they would try to geld St. Mawr--to make him a gelding?" Lewis looked up at her. There was a faint deadly glimmer of contempt on his face.

"Very likely, Mam," he said.

She was afraid of his cold, uncanny pale eyes, with their uneasy grey dawn of contempt. These two men, with their silent, deadly inner purpose, were not like other men. They seemed like two silent enemies of all the other men she knew. Enemies in the great white camp, disguised as servants, waiting the incalculable opportunity. What the opportunity might be, none knew.

"Sir Henry hasn't mentioned anything to me about selling St. Mawr to Miss Manby," she said.

The derisive flicker of a smile came on Phoenix's face.

"He sell him first, and tell you then," he said, with his deadly impassive manner.

"But do you really think so?" she asked.

It was extraordinary how much corrosive contempt Phoenix could convey, saying nothing. She felt it almost as an insult. Yet it was a relief to her.

"You know, I can't believe it. I can't believe Sir Henry would want to have St. Mawr mutilated. I believe he'd rather shoot him."

"You think so?" said Phoenix, with a faint grin.

Lou turned to Lewis.

"Lewis, will you tell me what you truly think?"

Lewis looked at her with a hard, straight, fearless British stare.

"That man Philips was in the 'Moon and Stars' last night. He said Miss Manby told him she was buying St. Mawr, and she asked him if he thought it would be safe to cut him and make a horse of him. He said it would be better, take some of the nonsense out of him. He's no good for a sire, anyhow--"

Lewis dropped his head again, and tapped a tattoo with the toe of his rather small foot.

"And what do you think?" said Lou. It occurred to her how sensible and practical Miss Manby was, so much more so than the Dean.

Lewis looked up at her with his pale eyes.

"It won't have anything to do with me," he said. "I shan't go to Corrabach Hall."

"What will you do, then?"

Lewis did not answer. He looked at Phoenix.

"Maybe him and me go to America," said Phoenix, looking at the void.

"Can he get in?" said Lou.

"Yes, he can. I know how," said Phoenix.

"And the money?" she said.

"We got money."

There was a silence, after which she asked of Lewis: "You'd leave St. Mawr to his fate?"

"I can't help his fate," said Lewis. "There's too many people In the world for me to help anything."

"Poor St. Mawr!"

She went indoors again and up to her room: then higher, to the top rooms of the tall Georgian house. From one window she could see the fields in the rain. She could see St. Mawr himself, alone as usual, standing with his head up, looking across the fences. He was streaked dark with rain. Beautiful, with his poised head and massive neck and his supple hindquarters. He was neighing to Poppy. Clear on the wet wind came the sound of his bell-like, stallion's calling, that Mrs. Vyner called cruel. It was a strange noise, with a splendour that belonged to another world age. The mean cruelty of Mrs. Vyner's humanitarianism, the barren cruelty of Flora Manby, the eunuch cruelty of Rico. Our whole eunuch civilisation, nasty-minded as eunuchs are, with their kind of sneaking, sterilising cruelty.

Yet even she herself, seeing St. Mawr's conceited march along the fence, could not help addressing him:

"Yes, my boy! If you knew what Miss Flora Manby was preparing for you! *She'll* sharpen a knife that will settle you." And Lou called her mother.

The two American women stood high at the window, overlooking the wet, close, hedged-and-fenced English landscape. Everything enclosed, enclosed, to stifling. The very apples on the trees looked so shut in, it was impossible to imagine any speck of 'Knowledge' lurking inside them. Good to eat, good to cook, good even for show. But the wild sap of untameable and inexhaustible knowledge--no! Bred out of them. Geldings, even the apples.

Mrs. Witt listened to Lou's half-humorous statements. "You must admit, mother, Flora is a sensible girl," she said.

"I admit it, Louise."

"She goes straight to the root of the matter."

"And eradicates the root. Wise girl! And what is your answer?"

"I don't know, mother. What would you say?"

"I know what I should say."

"Tell me."

"I should say: 'Miss Manby, you may have my husband, but not my horse. My husband won't need emasculating, and my horse I won't have you meddle, with. I'll preserve one last male thing in the museum of this world, if I can.'"

Lou listened, smiling faintly.

"That's what I will say," she replied at length. "The funny thing is, mother, they think all their men with their bare faces or their little quotation-mark moustaches are so tremendously male. That fox-hunting one!"

"I know it. Like little male motor-cars. Give him a little gas, and start him on the low gear, and away he goes: all his male gear rattling, like a cheap motor-car."

"I'm afraid I dislike men altogether, mother."

"You may, Louise. Think of Flora Manby, and how you love the fair sex."

"After all, St. Mawr is better. And I'm glad if he gives them a kick in the face."

"Ah, Louise!" Mrs. Witt suddenly clasped her hands with wicked passion. "*Ay, qué gozo!* as our Juan used to say, on your father's ranch in Texas." She gazed in a sort of wicked ecstasy out of the window.

They heard Lou's maid softly calling Lady Carrington from below. Lou went to the stairs.

"What is it?"

"Lewis want to speak to you, my Lady."

"Send him into the sitting-room."

The two women went down.

"What is it, Lewis?" asked Lou.

"Am I to bring in St. Mawr, in case they send for him from Corrabach?"

"No," said Lou swiftly.

"Wait a minute," put in Mrs. Witt. "What makes you think they will send for St. Mawr from Corrabach, Lewis?" she asked, suave as a grey leopard cat.

"Miss Manby went up to Flints Farm with Dean Vyner this morning, and they've just come back. They stopped the car, and Miss Manby got out at the field gate to look at St. Mawr. I'm thinking, if she made the bargain with Sir Henry, she'll be sending a man over this afternoon, and if I'd better brush tit. Mawr down a bit, in case."

The man stood strangely still, and the words came like shadows of his real meaning. It was a challenge.

"I see," said Mrs. Witt slowly.

Lou's face darkened. She, too, saw.

"So that is her game," she said. "That is why they got me down here."

"Never mind, Louise," said Mrs. Witt. Then to Lewis: "Yes, please bring in St. Mawr. You wish it, don't you, Louise?"

"Yes," hesitated Lou. She saw by Mrs. Witt's closed face that a counter-move was prepared.

"And Lewis," said Mrs. Witt, "my daughter may wish you to ride St. Mawr this afternoon--not to Corrabach Hall."

"Very good, Mam."

Mrs. Witt sat silent for some time, after Lewis had gone, gathering inspiration from the wet, grisly grave-stones.

"Don't you think it's time we made a move, daughter?" she asked.

"Any move," said Lou desperately.

"Very well then. My dearest friends, and my *only* friends, in this country, are in Oxfordshire. I will set off to *ride* to Merriton this afternoon, and Lewis will ride with me on St. Mawr."

"But you can't ride to Merriton in an afternoon," said Lou.

"I know it. I shall ride across country. I shall *enjoy* it, Louise.--Yes.--I shall consider I am on my way back to America. I am most deadly tired of this country. From Merriton I shall make my arrangements to go to America, and take Lewis and Phoenix and St. Mawr along with me. I think they want to go.--You will decide for yourself."

"Yes, I'll come too," said Lou casually.

"Very well. I'll start immediately after lunch, for I can't breathe in this place any longer. Where are Henry's automobile maps?"

Afternoon saw Mrs. Witt, in a large waterproof cape, mounted on her horse, Lewis, in another cape, mounted on St. Mawr, trotting through the rain, splashing in the puddles, moving slowly southwards. They took the open country, and would pass quite close to Flints Farm. But Mrs. Witt did not care. With great difficulty she had managed to fasten a small waterproof roll behind her, containing her night things. She seemed to breathe the first breath of freedom.

And sure enough, an hour or so after Mrs. Witt's departure, arrived Flora Manby in a splashed-up motor-car, accompanied by her sister, and bringing a groom and a saddle.

"Do you know, Harry sold me St. Mawr," she said. "I' just wild to get that horse in hand."

"How?" said Lou.

"Oh, I don't know. There are ways. Do you mind if Philips rides him over now to Corrabach?--0h, I forgot, Harry sent you a note:

"Dearest Loulina: Have you been gone from here two days or two years? It seems the latter. You are terribly missed. Flora wanted so much to buy St. Mawr, to save us further trouble, that I have sold him to her. She is giving me what we paid: rather, what you paid, so of course the money is yours. I am thankful we are rid of the animal, and that he falls into competent hands--I asked her please to remove him from your charge to-day. And I can't tell how much easier I am in my mind, to think of him gone. You are coming back to me to-morrow, aren't you? I shall think of nothing but you, till I see you. Arrivederci, darling dear! R."

"I'm so sorry," said Lou. "Mother went on horseback to see some friends, and Lewis went with her on St. Mawr. He knows the road."

"She'll be back this evening?" said Flora.

"I don't know. Mother is so uncertain. She may be away a day or two."

"Well, here's the cheque for St. Mawr."

"No, I won't take it now--no, thank you--not till mother comes back with the goods."

Flora was chagrined. The two women knew they hated one another. The visit was a brief one.

Mrs. Witt rode on in the rain, which abated as the afternoon wore down, and the evening came without rain, and with a suffusion of pale yellow light. All the time she had trotted in silence, with Lewis just behind her. And she scarcely saw the heather-covered hills with the deep clefts between them, nor the oak woods, nor the lingering foxgloves, nor the earth at all. Inside herself she felt a profound repugnance for the English country: she preferred even the crudeness of Central Park in New York.

And she felt an almost savage desire to get away from Europe, from everything European. Now she was really en route, she cared not a straw for St. Mawr or for Lewis or anything. Something just writhed inside her, all the time, against Europe. That closeness, that sense of cohesion, that sense of being fused into a lump with all the rest--no matter how much distance you kept--this drove her mad. In America the cohesion was a matter of choice and will. But in Europe it was organic, like the helpless particles of one sprawling body. And the great body in a state of incipient decay.

She was a woman of fifty-one: and she seemed hardly to have lived a day. She looked behind her--the thin trees and swamps of Louisiana, the sultry, sub-tropical excitement of decaying New Orleans, the vast bare dryness of Texas, with mobs of cattle in an illumined dust! The half-European thrills of New York! The false stability of Boston! A clever husband, who was a brilliant lawyer, but who was far more thrilled by his cattle ranch than by his law: and who drank heavily and died. The years of first widowhood in Boston, consoled by a self-satisfied sort of intellectual courtship from clever men.--For curiously enough, while she wanted it, she had always been able to compel men to pay court to her. All kinds of men.--Then a rather dashing time in New York--when she was in her early forties. Then the long visual, philandering in Europe. She left off 'loving', save through the eye, when she came to Europe. And when she made her trips to America, she found it was finished there also, her 'loving'.

What was the matter? Examining herself, she had long ago decided that her nature was a destructive force. But then, she justified herself, she had only destroyed that which was destructible. If she could have found something indestructible, especially in men, though she would have fought against it, she would have been glad at last to be defeated by it.

That was the point. She really wanted to be defeated, in her own eyes. And nobody had ever defeated her. Men were never really her match. A woman of terrible strong health, she felt even that in her strong limbs there was far more electric power than in the limbs of any man she had met. That curious fluid electric force, that could make any man kiss her hand, if she so willed it. A queen, as far as she wished. And not having been very clever at school, she always had the greatest respect for the mental powers. Her own were not mental powers. Rather electric, as of some strange physical dynamo within her. So she had been ready to bow before Mind.

But alas! After a brief time, she had found Mind, at least the man who was supposed to have the mind, bowing before her. Her own peculiar dynamic force was stronger than the force of Mind. She could make Mind kiss her hand.

And not by any sensual tricks. She did not really care about sensualities, especially as a younger woman. Sex was a mere adjunct. She cared about the mysterious, intense, dynamic sympathy that could flow between her and some 'live' man--a man who was highly conscious, a real live wire. That she cared about.

But she had never rested until she had made the man she admired--and admiration was the roots of her attraction to any man--made him kiss her hand. In both cases, actual and metaphorical. Physical and metaphysical. Conquered his country.

She had always succeeded. And she believed that, if she cared, she always would succeed. In the world of living men. Because of the power that was in her, in her arms, in her strong, shapely, but terrible hands, in all the great dynamo of her body.

For this reason she had been so terribly contemptuous of Rico, and of Lou's infatuation. Ye gods! what was Rico in the scale of men!

Perhaps she despised the younger generation too easily. Because she did not see its sources of power, she concluded it was powerless. Whereas perhaps the power of accommodating oneself to any circumstance and committing oneself to no circumstance is the last triumph of mankind.

Her generation had had its day. She had had her day. The world of her men had sunk into a sort of insignificance. And with a great contempt she despised the world that had come into place instead: the world of Rico and Flora Manby, the world represented, to her, by the Prince of Wales.

In such a world there was nothing even to conquer. It gave everything and gave nothing to everybody and anybody all the time. Dio Benedetto! as Rico would say. A great complicated tangle of nonentities ravelled in nothingness. So it seemed to her.

Great God! This was the generation she had helped to bring into the world.

She had had her day. And, as far as the mysterious battle of life went, she had won all the way. Just as Cleopatra, in the mysterious business of a woman's life, won all the way. Though that bald, tough Caesar had drawn his iron from the fire without losing much of its temper. And he had gone his way. And Antony surely was splendid to die with.

In her life there had been no tough Caesar to go his way in cold blood, away from her. Her men had gone from her like dogs on three legs, into the crowd. And certainly there was no gorgeous Antony to die for and with.

Almost she was tempted in her heart to cry: "Conquer me, oh God, before I die!'--But then she had a terrible contempt for the God that was supposed to rule this universe. She felt she could make *Him* kiss her hand. Here she was a woman of fifty-one, past the change of life. And her great dread was to die an empty, barren death. Oh, if only Death might open dark wings of mystery and consolation. To die an easy, barren death. To pass out as she had passed in, without mystery or the rustling of darkness! That was her last, final, ashy dread.

"Old!" she said to herself. "I am not *old!* I have lived many years, that is all. But I am as timeless as an hour-glass that turns morning and night, and spills the hours of sleep one way, the hours of consciousness the other way, without itself being affected. Nothing in all my life has ever truly affected me.--I believe Cleopatra only tried the asp, as she tried her pearls in wine, to see if it would really, really have any effect on her. Nothing had ever really had any effect on her, neither Caesar nor Antony nor any of them. Never once had she really been lost, lost to herself. Then try death, see if that trick would work. If she would lose herself to herself that way.--Ah, death--!"

But Mrs. Witt mistrusted death too. She felt she might pass out as a bed of asters passes out in autumn, to mere nothingness.--And something in her longed to die, at least, *positively:* to be folded then at last into throbbing wings of mystery, like, a hawk that goes to sleep. Not like a thing made into a parcel and put into the last rubbish-heap.

So she rode trotting across the hills, mile after mile, in silence. Avoiding the roads, avoiding everything, avoiding everybody, just trotting forwards, towards night.

And by nightfall they had travelled twenty-five miles. She had motored around this country, and knew the little towns and the inns. She knew where she would sleep.

The morning came beautiful and sunny. A woman so strong in health, why should she ride with the fact of death before her eyes? But she did.

Yet in sunny morning she must do something about it.

"Lewis!" she said. "Come here and tell me something, please! Tell me," she said, "do you believe in God?"

"In God!" he said, wondering. "I never think about it."

"But do you say your prayers?"

"No, Mam!"

"Why don't you?"

He thought about it for some minutes.

"I don't like religion. My aunt and uncle were religious."

"You don't like religion," she repeated. "And you don't believe in God.--Well, then--"

"Nay!" he hesitated. "I never said I didn't believe in God.--Only I'm sure I'm not a Methodist. And I feel a fool in a proper church.--And I feel a fool saying my prayers.--And I feel a fool when ministers and parsons come getting at me.--I never think about God, if folks don't try to make me." He had a small, sly smile, almost gay.

"And you don't like feeling a fool?" She smiled rather patronisingly.

"No, Mam."

"Do I make you feel a fool?" she asked dryly.

He looked at her without answering.

"Why don't you answer?" she said, pressing.

"I think you'd like to make a fool of me sometimes," he said. "Now?" she pressed.

He looked at her with that slow, distant look.

"Maybe!" he said, rather unconcernedly.

Curiously, she couldn't touch him. He always seemed to be watching her from a distance, as if from another country. Even if she made a fool of him, something in him would all the time be far away from her, not implicated.

She caught herself up in the personal game and returned to her own isolated question. A vicious habit made her start the personal tricks. She didn't want to, really.

There was something about this little man--sometimes, to herself, she called him *Little Jack Horner, sat in a corner*--that irritated her and made her want to taunt him. His peculiar little inaccessibility, that was so tight and easy.

Then again, there was something, his way of looking at her as if he looked from out of another country, a country of which he was an inhabitant, and where she had never been: this touched her strangely. Perhaps behind this little man was the mystery. In spite of the fact that in actual life, in her world, he was only a groom, almost *chétif*, with his legs a little bit horsy and bowed; and of no education, saying 'Yes, Mam!' and 'No, Mam!' and accomplishing nothing, simply nothing at all on the face of the earth. Strictly a nonentity.

And yet, what made him perhaps the only real entity to her, his seeming to inhabit another world than hers. A world dark and still, where language never ruffled the growing leaves and seared their edges like a bad wind.

Was it an illusion, however? Sometimes she thought it was. Just bunkum, which she had faked up, in order to have something to mystify about.

But then, when she saw Phoenix and Lewis silently together, she knew there *was* another communion, silent, excluding her. And sometimes when Lewis was alone with St. Mawr: and once when she saw him pick up a bird that had stunned itself against a wire: she had realised another world, silent, where each creature is alone in its own aura of silence, the mystery of power: as Lewis had power with St. Mawr, and even with Phoenix.

The visible world and the invisible. Or rather, the audible and the inaudible. She had lived so long, and so completely, in the visible, audible world. She would not easily admit that other, inaudible. She always wanted to jeer as she approached the brink of it.

Even now she wanted to jeer at the little fellow, because of his holding himself inaccessible within the inaudible, silent world. And she knew he knew it.

"Did you never want to be rich, and be a gentleman, like Sir Henry?" she asked.

"I would many times have liked to be rich. But I never exactly wanted to be a gentleman," he said.

"Why not?"

"I can't exactly say. I should be uncomfortable if I was like they are."

"And are you comfortable now?"

"When I'm let alone."

"And do they let you alone? Does the world let you alone?"

"No, they don't."

"Well then--!"

"I keep to myself all I can."

"And are you comfortable, as you call it, when you keep to yourself?"

"Yes, I am."

"But when you keep to yourself, what do you keep to? What precious treasure have you to keep to?"

He looked, and saw she was jeering.

"None," he said. "I've got nothing of that sort."

She rode impatiently on ahead.

And the moment she had done so, she regretted it. She might put the little fellow, with contempt, out of her reckoning. But no, she would not do it.

She had put so much out of her reckoning: soon she would be left in an empty circle, with her empty self at the centre. She reined in again.

"Lewis!" she said. "I don't want you to take offence at anything I say."

"No, Mam."

"I don't want you to say just 'No, Mam!' all the time!" she cried impulsively. "Promise me."

"Yes, Mam!"

"But really! Promise me you won't be offended at whatever I say."

"Yes, Mam!"

She looked at him searchingly. To her surprise, she was almost in tears. A woman of her years! And with a servant!

But his face was blank and stony, with a stony, distant look of pride that made him inaccessible to her emotions. He met her eyes again: with that cold distant look, looking straight into her hot, confused, pained self. So cold and as if merely refuting her. He didn't believe her, nor trust her, nor like her even. She was an attacking enemy to him. Only he stayed really far away from her, looking down at her from a sort of distant hill where her weapons could not reach: not quite.

And at the same time, it hurt him in a dumb, living way, that she made these attacks on him. She could see the cloud of hurt in his eyes, no matter how distantly he looked at her.

They bought food in a village shop, and sat under a tree near a field where men were already cutting oats, in a warm valley. Lewis had stabled the horses for a couple of hours to feed and rest. But he came to join her under the tree, to eat.--He sat a little distance from her, with the bread and cheese in his small brown hands, eating silently, and watching the harvesters. She was cross with him, and therefore she was stingy, would give him nothing to eat but dry bread and cheese. Herself, she was not hungry.--So all the time he kept his face a little averted from her. As a matter of fact, he kept his whole being averted from her, away from her. He did not want to touch her, nor to be touched by her. He kept his spirit there, alert, on its guard, but out of contact. It was as if he had unconsciously accepted the battle, the old battle. He was her target, the old object of her deadly weapons. But he refused to shoot back. It was as if he caught all her missiles in full flight before they touched him, and silently threw them on the ground behind him. And in some essential part of himself he ignored her, staying in another world.

That other world! Mere male armour of artificial imperviousness! It angered her.

Yet she knew, by the way he watched the harvesters, and the grasshoppers popping into notice, that it was another world. And when a girl went by, carrying food to the field, it was at him she glanced. And he gave that quick, animal little smile that came from him unawares. Another world.

Yet also there was a sort of meanness about him: a *suffisance!* A keep-yourself-for-yourself, and don't give yourself away.

Well!--she rose impatiently.

It was hot in the afternoon, and she was rather tired. She went to the inn and slept, and did not start again till tea-time. Then they had to ride rather late. The sun sank, among a smell of cornfields, clear and yellow-red behind motionless dark trees. Pale smoke rose from cottage chimneys. Not a cloud was in the sky, which held the upward-floating light like a bowl inverted on purpose. A new moon sparkled and was gone. It was beginning of night.

Away in the distance, they saw a curious pinkish glare of fire, probably furnaces. And Mrs. Witt thought she could detect the scent of furnace smoke, or factory smoke. But then she always said that of the English air: it was never quite free of the smell of smoke, coal smoke.

They were riding slowly on a path through fields, down a long slope. Away below was a puther of lights. All the darkness seemed full of half-spent crossing lights, a curious uneasiness. High in the sky a star seemed to be walking. It was an aeroplane with a light. Its buzz rattled above. Not a space, not a speck of this country that wasn't humanised, occupied by the human claim. Not even the sky.

They descended slowly through a dark wood, which they had entered through a gate. Lewis was all the time dismounting and opening gates, letting her pass, shutting the gate and mounting again.

So, in a while she came to the edge of the wood's darkness, and saw the open pale concave of the world beyond. The darkness was never dark. It shook with the concussion of many invisible lights, lights of towns, villages, mines, factories, furnaces, squatting in the valleys and behind all the hills.

Yet, as Rachel Witt drew rein at the gate emerging from the wood, a very big, soft star fell in heaven, cleaving the hubbub of this human night with a gleam from the greater world.

"See! a star falling!" said Lewis, as he opened the gate.

"I saw it," said Mrs. Witt, walking her horse past him.

There was a curious excitement of wonder, or magic, in the little man's voice. Even in this night something strange had stirred awake in him.

"You ask me about God," he said to her, walking his horse alongside in the shadow of the wood's edge, the darkness of the old Pan, that kept our artificial-ly-lit world at bay. "I don't know about God. But when I see a star fall like that out of long-distance places in the sky: and the moon sinking saying Good-bye! Good-bye! Good-bye! and nobody listening: I think I hear something, though I wouldn't call it God."

"What then?" said Rachel Witt.

"And you smell the smell of oak leaves now," he said, "now the air is cold. They smell to me more alive than people. The trees hold their bodies hard and still, but they watch and listen with their leaves. And I think they say to me: 'Is that you passing there, Morgan Lewis? All right, you pass quickly, we shan't do anything to you. You are like a holly bush.'"

"Yes," said Rachel Witt dryly. "Why?"

"All the time the trees grow and listen. And if you cut a tree down without asking pardon, trees will hurt you sometime in your life, in the night-time."

"I suppose," said Rachel Witt, "that's an old superstition."

"They say that ash trees don't like people. When the other people were most in the country--I mean like what they call fairies, that have all gone now--they liked ash trees best. And you know the little green things with little small nuts in them, that come flying from ash trees--*pigeons*, we call them--they're the seeds--the other people used to catch them and eat them before they fell to the ground. And that made the people so they could hear trees living and feeling things.--But when all these people that there are now came to England, they liked the oak trees best, because their pigs ate the acorns. So now you can tell the ash trees are mad, they want to kill all these people. But the oak trees are many more than the ash trees."

"And do you eat the ash tree seeds?" she asked.

"I always ate them when I was little. Then I wasn't frightened of ash trees, like most of the others. And I wasn't frightened of the moon. If you didn't go near the fire all day, and if you didn't eat any cooked food nor anything that had been in the sun, but only things like turnips or radishes or pignuts, and then went without any clothes on, in the full moon, then you could see the people in the moon, and go with them. They never have fire, and they never speak, and their bodies are clear almost like jelly. They die in a minute if there's a bit of fire near them. But they know more than we. Because unless fire touches them, they never die. They see people live and they see people perish, and they say, people are only like twigs on a tree, you break them off the tree, and kindle fire with them. You made a fire of them, and they are gone, the fire is gone, everything is gone. But the people of the moon don't die, and fire is nothing to them. They look at it from the distance of the sky, and see it burning things up, people all appearing and disappearing like twigs that come in spring and you cut them in autumn and make a fire of them and they are gone. And they say: What do people matter? If you want to matter, you must become a moon-boy. Then all your life, fire can't blind you and people can't hurt you. Because at full moon you can join the moon people, and go through the air and pass any cool places, pass through rocks and through the trunks of trees, and when you come to people lying warm in bed, you punish them."

"How?"

"You sit on' the pillow where they breathe, and you put a web across their mouth, so they can't breathe the fresh air that comes from the moon. So they go on breathing the same air again and again, and that makes them more and more stupefied. The sun gives out heat, but the moon gives out fresh air. That's what the moon people do: they wash the air clean with moonlight."

He was talking with a strange, eager *naïveté* that amused Rachel Witt, and made her a little uncomfortable in her skin. Was he after all no more than a sort of imbecile?

"Who told you all this stuff?" she asked abruptly.

And, as abruptly, he pulled himself up.

"We used to say it when we were children."

"But you don't believe it? It is only childishness, after all." He paused a moment or two.

"No," he said, in his ironical little day voice. "I know I shan't make anything but a fool of myself, with that talk. But all sorts of things go through our heads, and some seem to linger, and some don't. But you asking me about God put it into my mind, I suppose. I don't know what sort of things I believe in: only I know it's not what the chapel folks believe in. We none of us believe in them when it comes to earning a living, or, with you people, when it comes to spending your fortune. Then we know that bread costs money, and even your sleep you have to pay for.--That's work. Or, with you people, it's just owning property and seeing you get your value for your money.--But a man's mind is always full of things. And some people's minds, like my aunt and uncle, are full of religion and hell for everybody except themselves. And some people's minds are all money, money, money, and how to get hold of something they haven't got hold of yet. And some people, like you, are always curious about what everybody else in the world is after. And some people are all for enjoying themselves and being thought much of, and some, like Lady Carrington, don't know what to do with themselves. Myself, I don't want to have in my mind the things other people have in their minds. I'm one that likes my own things best. And if, when I see a bright star fall, like to-night, I think to myself: 'There's movement in the sky. The world is going to change again. They're throwing something to us from the distance, and we've got to have it, whether we want it or not. To-morrow there will be a difference for everybody, thrown out of the sky upon us, whether we want it or not: then that's how I want to think, so let me please myself.'"

"You know what a shooting star actually is, I suppose?--and that there are always many in August, because we pass through a region of them?"

"Yes, Mam, I've been told. But stones don't come at us from the sky for nothing. Either it's like when a man tosses an apple to you out of his orchard, as you go by. Or it's like when somebody shies a stone at you to cut your head open. You'll never make me believe the sky is like an empty house with a slate falling from the roof. The world has its own life, the sky has a life of its own, and never is it like stones rolling down a rubbish-heap and falling into a pond. Many things twitch and twitter within the sky, and many things happen beyond us. My own way of thinking is my own way."

"I never knew you talk so much."

"No, Mam. It's your asking me that about God. Or else it's the night-time. I don't believe in God and being good and going to heaven. Neither do I worship idols, so I'm not a heathen as my aunt called me. Never from a boy did I want to believe the things they kept grinding in their guts at home, and at Sunday school, and at school. A man's mind has to be full of something, so I keep to what we used to think as lads. It's childish nonsense, I know it. But it suits me. Better than other people's stuff. Your man Phoenix is about the same, when he lets on.--Anyhow, it's my own stuff that we believed as lads, and I like it better than other people's stuff.--You asking about God made me let on. But I would never belong to any club, or trades union, and God's the same to my mind."

With this he gave a little kick to his horse, and St. Mawr went dancing excitedly along the highway they now entered, leaving Mrs. Witt to trot after as rapidly as she could.

When she came to the hotel, to which she had telegraphed for rooms, Lewis disappeared, and she was left thinking hard.

It was not till they were twenty miles from Merriton, riding through a slow morning mist, and she had a rather far-away, wistful look on her face, unusual for her, that she turned to him in the saddle and said:

"Now don't be surprised, Lewis, at what I am going to say. I am going to ask you, now, supposing I wanted to marry you, what should you say?"

He looked at her quickly, and was at once on his guard. "That you didn't mean it," he replied hastily.

"Yes"--she hesitated, and her face looked wistful and tired.--"Supposing I *did* mean it. Supposing I did *really*, from my heart, want to marry you and be a wife to you"--she looked away across the fields--"then what should you say?"

Her voice sounded sad, a little broken.

"Why, Mam!" he replied, knitting his brow and shaking his head a little. "I should say you didn't mean it, you know. Something would have come over you."

"But supposing I *wanted* something to come over me?" He shook his head.

"It would never do, Mam Some people's flesh and blood is kneaded like bread: and that's me. And some are rolled like fine pastry, like Lady Carrington. And some are mixed with gunpowder. They're like a cartridge you put in a gun, Mam."

She listened impatiently.

"Don't talk," she said, "about bread and cakes and pastry, it all means nothing. You used to answer short enough 'Yes, Mam! No, Mam!' That will do now. Do you mean 'Yes!' or 'No!?'"

His eyes met hers. She was again hectoring.

"No, Mam!" he said, quite neutral. "Why?"

As she waited for his answer, she saw the foundations of his loquacity dry up, his face go distant and mute again, as it always used to be, till these last two days, when it had had a funny touch of inconsequential merriness.

He looked steadily into her eyes, and his look was neutral, sombre, and hurt. He looked at her as if infinite seas, infinite spaces divided him and her. And his eyes seemed to put her away beyond some sort of fence. An anger congealed cold like lava, set impassive against her and all her sort.

"No, Mam. I couldn't give my body to any woman who didn't respect it."

"But I do respect it, I do!"--she flushed hot like a girl.

"No, Mam. Not as *I* mean it," he replied.

There was a touch of anger against her in his voice, and a distance of distaste.

"And how do you mean it?" she replied, the full sarcasm coming back into her tones. She could see that, as a woman to touch and fondle he saw her as repellent: only repellent.

"I have to be a servant to women now," he said, "even to earn my wage. I could never touch with my body a woman whose servant I was."

"You're not my servant: my daughter pays your wages.--And all that is beside the point, between a man and a woman."

"No woman who I touched with my body should ever speak to me as you speak to me, or think of me as you think of me," he said.

"But!--" she stammered. "I think of you--with love. And can you be so unkind as to notice the way I speak? You know it's only my way."

"You, as a woman," he said, "you have no respect for a man."

"Respect! Respect!" she cried. "I'm likely to lose what respect I have left. I know I can *love* a man. But whether a man can love a woman--"

"No," said Lewis. "I never could, and I think I never shall. Because I don't want to. The thought of it makes me feel shame."

"What do you mean" she cried.

"Nothing in the world," he said, "would make me feel such shame as to have a woman shouting at me, or mocking at me, as I see women mocking and despising the men they marry. No woman shall touch my body and mock me or despise me. No woman."

"But men must be mocked, or despised even, sometimes."

"No. Not this man. Not by the woman I touch with my body."

"Are you perfect?"

"I don't know. But if I touch a woman with my body, it must put a lock on her, to respect what I will never have despised: never!"

"What will you never have despised?"

"My body! And my touch upon the woman."

"Why insist so on your body?"--And she looked at him with a touch of contemptuous mockery, raillery.

He looked her in the eyes steadily, and coldly, putting her away from him, and himself far away from her.

"Do you expect that any woman still stay your humble slave to-day?" she asked cuttingly.

But he only watched her coldly, distant, refusing any connection.

"Between men and women, it's a question of give and take. A man can't expect *always* to be humbly adored."

He watched her still, cold, rather pale, putting her far from him. Then he turned his horse and set off rapidly along the road, leaving her to follow.

She walked her horse and let him go, thinking to herself: "There's a little bantam cock. And a groom! Imagine it! Thinking he can dictate to a woman!"

She was in love with him. And he, in an odd way, was in love with her. She had known it by the odd, uncanny merriment in him, and his unexpected loquacity. But he would not have her come physically near him. Unapproachable there as a cactus, guarding his 'body' from her contact. As if contact with her would be mortal insult and fatal injury to his marvellous 'body'.

What a little cock-sparrow!

Let him ride ahead. He would have to wait for her somewhere.

She found him at the entrance to the next village. His face was pallid and set. She could tell he felt he had been insulted, so he had congealed into stiff insentience.

"At the bottom of all men is the same," she said to herself: "an empty, male conceit of themselves."

She, too, rode up with a face like a mask, and straight on to the hotel.

"Can you serve dinner to myself and my servant?" she asked at the inn: which, fortunately for her, accommodated motorists, otherwise they would have said 'No!'

"I think," said Lewis as they came in sight of Merriton, "I'd better give Lady Carrington a week's notice."

A complete little stranger! And an impudent one. "Exactly as you please," she said.

She found several letters from her daughter at Marshal Place. "Dear Mother: No sooner had you gone off than Flora appeared, not at all in the bud, but rather in full blow. She demanded her victim; Shylock demanding the pound of flesh: and wanted to hand over the shekels.

"Joyfully I refused them. She said 'Harry' was much better, and invited him and me to stay at Corrabach Hall till he was quite well: it would be less strain on your household, while he was still in bed and helpless. So the plan is, that he shall be brought down on Friday, if he is really fit for the journey, and we drive straight to Corrabach. I am packing his bags and mine, clearing up our traces: his trunks to go to Corrabach, mine to stay here and make up their minds.--I am going to Flints Farm again to-morrow, dutifully, though I am no flower for the bedside.--I do so want to know if Rico has already called her Fiorita: or perhaps Florecita. It reminds me of old William's joke: 'Now yuh tell me, little Missy: which is the best posey that grow?' And the hushed whisper in which he said the answer: 'The Collyposy!' Oh dear, I am so tired of feeling spiteful, but how else is one to feel?

"You looked most prosaically romantic, setting off in a rubber cape, followed by Lewis. Hope the roads were not very slippery, and that you had a good time, *à la Mademoiselle de Maupin*. Do remember, dear, not to devour little Lewis before you have got half-way--"

"Dear Mother: I half expected word from you before I left, but nothing came. Forrester drove me up here just before lunch. Rico seems much better, almost himself, and a little more than that. He broached our staying at Corrabach very tactfully. I told him Flora had asked me, and it seemed a good plan. Then I told him about St. Mawr. He was a little piqued, and there was a pause of very disapproving silence. Then he said: 'Very well, darling. If you wish to keep the animal, do so by all means. I make a present of him again.' Me: 'That's so good of you, Rico. Because I know revenge is sweet.' Rico: 'Revenge, Loulina! I don't think I was selling him for vengeance! Merely to get rid of him to Flora, who can keep better hold over him.' Me: 'But you know, dear, she was going to geld him!' Rico: 'I don't think anybody knew it. We only wondered if it were possible, to make him more amenable. Did she tell you?' Me: 'No--Phoenix did. He had it from a groom.' Rico: 'Dear me! A concatenation of grooms! So your mother rode off with Lewis, and carried St. Mawr out of danger! I understand! Let us hope worse won't befall.' Me: 'Whom?' Rico: 'Never mind, dear! It's so lovely to see you. You are looking rested. I thought those Countess of Wilton roses the most marvellous things in the world, till you came, now they're quite in the background.' He had some very lovely roses in a crystal bowl: the room smelled of roses. Me: 'Where did they come from?' Rico: 'Oh, Flora brought them!' Me: 'Bowl and all?' Rico: 'Bowl and all! Wasn't it dear of her?' Me: 'Why, yes! But then she's the goddess of flowers, isn't she?' Poor darling, he was offended that I should twit him while he is ill, so I relented. He has had a couple of marvellous invalid's bed-jackets sent from London: one a pinkish yellow, with rose-arabesque facings: this one in fine cloth. But unfortunately he has already dropped soup on it. The other is a lovely silvery and blue and green, soft brocade. He had that one on to receive me, and I at once complimented him on it. He has got a new ring too: sent by Aspasia Weingartner, a rather lovely intaglio of Priapus under an apple bough, at least, so he says it is. He made a naughty face, and said: 'The Priapus stage is rather advanced for poor me.' I asked what the Priapus stage was, but he said: 'Oh, nothing!' Then nurse said: 'There's a big classical dictionary that Miss Manby brought up, if you wish to see it.' So I have been studying the Classical Gods. The world always was a queer place. It's a very queer one when Rico is the god Priapus. He would go round the orchard painting life-like apples on the trees, and inviting nymphs to come and eat them. And the nymphs would pretend they were real: 'Why, Sir Prippy, what stunningly naughty apples!' There's nothing so artificial as sinning nowadays. I suppose it once was real.

"I'm bored here: wish I had my horse."

"Dear Mother: I'm so glad you are enjoying your ride. I'm sure it is like riding into history, like the Yankee at the Court of King Arthur, in those old by-lanes and Roman roads. They still fascinate me: at least, more before I get there than when I am actually there. I begin to feel real American and to resent the past. Why doesn't the past decently bury itself instead of waiting to be admired by the present?

"Phoenix brought Poppy. I am so fond of her: rode for five hours yesterday. I was glad to get away from this farm. The doctor came, and said Rico would be able to go down to Corrabach to-morrow. Flora came to hear the bulletin, and sailed back full of zest. Apparently Rico is going to do a portrait of her, sitting up in bed. What a mercy the bedclothes won't be mine when Priapus wields his palette from the pillow.

"Phoenix thinks you intend to go to America with St. Mawr, and that I am coming too, leaving Rico this side.--I wonder. I feel so unreal, nowadays, as if I too were nothing more than a painting by Rico on a millboard. I feel almost too unreal even to make up my mind to anything. It is terrible when the life-flow dies out of one, and everything is like cardboard, and oneself is like cardboard. I'm sure it is worse than being dead. I realised it yesterday when Phoenix and I had a picnic lunch by a stream. You see, I must imitate you in all things. He found me some watercresses, and they tasted so damp and alive, I knew how deadened I was. Phoenix wants us to go and have a ranch in Arizona, and raise horses, with St. Mawr, if willing, for Father Abraham. I wonder if it matters what one does: if it isn't all the same thing over again? Only Phoenix, his funny blank face, makes my heart melt and go sad. But I believe he'd be cruel too. I saw it in his face when he didn't know I was looking. Anything, though, rather than this deadness and this paint-Priapus business. *Au revoir*, mother dear! Keep on having a good time--"

"Dear Mother: I had your letter from Merriton: am so glad you arrived safe and sound in body and temper. There was such a funny letter from Lewis, too: I enclose it. What makes him take this extraordinary line? But I'm writing to tell him to take St. Mawr to London, and wait for me there. I have telegraphed Mrs. Squire to get the house ready for me. I shall go straight there.

"Things developed here, as they were bound to. I just couldn't bear it. No sooner was Rico put in the automobile than a self-conscious importance came over him, like when the wounded hero is carried into the middle of the stage. 'Why so solemn, Rico dear?' I asked him, trying to laugh him out of it. 'Not solemn, dear, only feeling a little transient.' I don't think he knew himself what he meant. Flora was on the steps as the car drew up, dressed in severe white. She only needed an apron to become a nurse: or a veil to become a bride. Between the two, she had an unbearable air of a woman in seduced circumstances, as The Times said. She ordered two menservants about in subdued, you would have said hushed, but competent tones. And then I saw there was a touch of the priestess about her as well: Cassandra preparing for her violation: Iphigenia, with Rico for Orestes, on a stretcher: he looking like Adonis, fully prepared to be an unconscionable time in dying. They had given him a lovely room downstairs, with doors opening on to a little garden all of its own. I believe it was Flora's boudoir. I left nurse and the men to put him to bed. Flora was hovering anxiously in the passage outside. 'Oh, what a marvellous room! Oh, how colourful, how beautiful!' came Rico's tones, the hero behind the scenes. I must say, it was like a harvest festival, with roses and gaillardias in the shadow, and cornflowers in the light, and a bowl of grapes, and nectarines among leaves. 'I'm so anxious that he should be happy,' Flora said to me in the passage. 'You know him best. Is there anything else I could do for him?' Me: 'Why, if you went to the piano and sang, I'm sure he'd love it. Couldn't you sing: Oh, my love is like a rred, rred rrose! '--You know how Rico imitates Scotch!

"Thank goodness I have a bedroom upstairs: nurse sleeps in a little ante-chamber to Rico's room. The Edwards are still here, the blond young man with some very futuristic plaster on his face. 'Awfully good of you to come!' he said to me, looking at me out of one eye, and holding my hand fervently. How's that for cheek: 'It's awfully good of Miss Manby to let me come,' said I. He: `Ah, but Flora is always a sport, a topping good sport!'

"I don't know what's the matter, but it just all put me into a fiendish temper. I felt I couldn't sit there at luncheon with that bright, youthful company, and hear about their tennis and their polo and their hunting and have their flirtatiousness making me sick. So I asked for a tray in my room. Do as I might, I couldn't help being horrid.

"Oh, and Rico! He really is too awful. Lying there in bed with every ear open, like Adonis waiting to be persuaded not to die. Seizing a hushed moment to take Flora's hand and press it to his lips, murmuring: 'How awfully good you are to me, dear Flora!' And Flora: 'I'd be better if I knew how, Harry!' So cheerful with it all! No, it's too much. My sense of humour is leaving me: which means, I'm getting into too bad a temper to be able to ridicule it all. I suppose I feel in the minority. It's an awful thought, to think that most all the young people in the world are like this: so bright and cheerful, and sporting, and so brimming with libido. How awful!

"I said to Rico: 'You're very comfortable here, aren't you?' He: 'Comfortable! It's comparative heaven.' Me: 'Would you mind if I went away?' A deadly pause. He is deadly afraid of being left alone with Flora. He feels safe so long as I am about, and he can take refuge in his marriage ties. He: 'Where do you want to go, dear?' Me: 'To mother. To London. Mother is planning to go to America, and she wants me to go.' Rico: 'But you don't want to go t--he--e--re--e I' You know, mother, how Rico can put a venomous emphasis on a word, till it suggests pure poison. It nettled me. `I'm not sure,' I said. Rico: 'Oh, but you can't stand that awful America.' Me: 'I want to try again.' Rico: 'But Lou dear, it will be winter before you get there. And this is absolutely the wrong moment for me to go over there. I am only just making headway over here. When I am absolutely sure of a position in England, then we nip across the Atlantic and scoop in a few dollars, if you like. Just now, even when I am well, would be fatal. I've only just sketched in the outline of my success in London, and one ought to arrive in New York ready-made as a famous and important Artist.' Me: 'But mother and I didn't think of going to New York. We thought we'd sail straight to New Orleans--if we could: or to Havana. And then go west to Arizona.' The poor boy looked at me in such distress. 'But Loulina darling, do you mean you want to leave me in the lurch for the winter season? You can't mean it. We're just getting on so splendidly, really!'--I was surprised at the depth of feeling in his voice: how tremendously his career as an artist--a popular artist--matters to him. I can never believe it.--You know, mother, you and I feel alike about daubing paint on canvas: every possible daub that can be daubed has already been done, so people ought to leave off. Rico is so shrewd. I always think he's got his tongue in his cheek, and I'm always staggered once more to find that he takes it absolutely seriously. His career! The Modern British Society of Painters: perhaps even the Royal Academy! Those people we see in London, and those portraits Rico does! He may even be a second Laszlo, or a thirteenth Orpen, and die happy! Oh! mother! How can it really matter to anybody!

"But I was really rather upset when I realised how his heart was fixed on his career, and that I might be spoiling everything for him. So I went away to think about it. And then I realised how unpopular you are, and how unpopular I shall be myself, in a little while. A sort of hatred for people has come over me. I hate their ways and their bunk, and I feel like kicking them in the face, as St. Mawr did that young man. Not that I should ever do it. And I don't think I should ever have made my final announcement to Rico, if he hadn't been such a beautiful pig in clover, here at Corrabach Hall. He has known the Manbys all his life; they and he are sections of one engine. He would be far happier with Flora: or I won't say happier, because there is something in him which rebels: but he would on the whole fit much better. I myself am at the end of my limit, and beyond it. I can't 'mix' any more, and I refuse to. I feel like a bit of egg-shell in the mayonnaise: the only thing is to take it out, you can't beat it in. I *know* I shall cause a fiasco, even in Rico's career, if I stay. I shall go on being rude and hateful to people as I am at Corrabach, and Rico will lose all his nerve.

"So I have told him. I said this evening, when no one was about: 'Rico dear, listen to me seriously. I can't stand these people. If you ask me to endure another week of them, I shall either become ill, or insult them, as mother does. And I don't want to do either.' Rico: 'But darling, isn't everybody perfect to you?' Me: 'I tell you, I shall just make a break, like St. Mawr, if I don't get out. I simply can't stand people.'--The poor darling, his face goes so blank and anxious. He knows what I mean, because, except that they tickle his vanity all the time, he hates them as much as I do. But his vanity is the chief thing to him. He: 'Lou darling, can't you wait till I get up, and we can go away to the Tyrol or somewhere for a spell?' Me: 'Won't you come with me to America, to the South-West? I believe it's marvellous country:--I saw his face switch into hostility; quite vicious. He: 'Are you so keen on spoiling everything for me? Is that what I married you for? Do you do it deliberately?' Me: 'Everything is already spoilt for me. I tell you I can't stand people, your Floras and your Aspasias, and your forthcoming young Englishmen. After all, I am an American, like mother, and I've got to go back.' He: 'Really! And am

I to come along as part of the luggage? Labelled cabin!' Me: 'You do as you wish, Rico.' He: 'I wish to God you did as you wished, Lou dear. I'm afraid you do as Mrs. Witt wishes. I always heard that the holiest thing in the world was a mother.' Me: 'No, dear, it's just that I can't stand people.' He (with a snarl): 'And I suppose I'm lumped in as PEOPLE!' And when he'd said it, it was true. We neither of us said anything for a time. Then he said, calculating: 'Very well, dear! You take a trip to the land of stars and stripes, and I'll stay here and go on with my work. And when you've seen enough of their stars and tasted enough of their stripes, you can come back and take your place again with me.'--We left it at that.

"You and I are supposed to have important business connected with our estates in Texas--it sounds so well--so we are making a hurried trip to the States, as they call them. I shall leave for London early next week--"

Mrs. Witt read this long letter with satisfaction. She herself had one strange craving: to get back to America. It was not that she idealised her native country: she was a tartar of restlessness there, quite as much as in Europe. It was not that she expected to arrive at any blessed abiding place. No, in America she would go on fuming and chafing the same. But at least she would be in America, in her own country. And that was what she wanted.

She picked up the sheet of poor paper that had been folded in Lou's letter. It was the letter from Lewis, quite nicely written. "Lady Carrington, I write to tell you and Sir Henry that I think I had better quit your service, as it would be more comfortable all round. If you will write and tell me what you want me to do with St. Mawr, I will do whatever you tell me. With kind regards to Lady Carrington and Sir Henry, I remain, Your obedient servant, Morgan Lewis."

Mrs. Witt put the letter aside, and sat looking out of the window. She felt, strangely, as if already her soul had gone away from her actual surroundings. She was there, in Oxfordshire, in the body, but her spirit had departed elsewhere. A listlessness was upon her. It was with an effort she roused herself, to write to her lawyer in London, to get her release from her English obligations. Then she wrote to the London hotel.

For the first time in her life she wished she had a maid to do little things for her. All her life she had had too much energy to endure anyone hanging round her, personally. Now she gave up. Her wrists seemed numb, as if the power in her were switched off.

When she went down they said Lewis had asked to speak to her. She had hardly seen him since they arrived at Merriton.

"I've had a letter from Lady Carrington, Mam. She says will I take St. Mawr to London and wait for her there. But she says I am to come to you, Mam, for definite orders."

"Very well, Lewis. I shall be going to London in a few days' time. You arrange for St. Mawr to go up one day this week, and you will take him to the Mews. Come to me for anything you want. And don't talk of leaving my daughter. We want you to go with St. Mawr to America, with us and Phoenix."

"And your horse, Mam?"

"I shall leave him here at Merriton. I shall give him to Miss Atherton."

"Very good, Mam!"

"Dear Daughter: I shall be in my old quarters in Mayfair next Saturday, calling the same day at your house to see if everything is ready for you. Lewis has fixed up with the railway: he goes to town to-morrow. The reason of his letter was that I had asked him if he would care to marry me, and he turned me down with emphasis. But I will tell you about it. You and I are the scribe and the Pharisee; I never could write a letter, and you could never leave off--"

"Dearest Mother: I smelt something rash, but I know it's no use saying: How *could* you? I only wonder, though, that you should think of marriage. You know, dear, I ache in every fibre to be left alone, from all that sort of thing. I feel all bruises, like one who has been assassinated. I do so understand why Jesus said: '*Noli me tangere.*' Touch me not, I am not yet ascended unto the Father. Everything had hurt him so much, wearied him so beyond endurance, he felt he could not bear one little human touch on his body. I am like that. I can hardly bear even Elena to hand me a dress. As for a man--and marriage--ah, no! *Noli me tangere, homine!* I am not yet ascended unto the Father. Oh, leave me alone, leave me alone! That is all my cry to all the world.

"Curiously, I feel that Phoenix understands what I feel. He leaves me so understandingly alone, he almost gives me my sheath of aloneness: or at least, he protects me in my sheath. I am grateful for him.

"Whereas Rico feels my aloneness as a sort of shame to himself. He wants at least a blinding pretence of intimacy. Ah, intimacy! The thought of it fills me with aches, and the pretence of it exhausts me beyond myself.

"Yes, I long to go away to the West, to be away from the world like one dead and in another life, in a valley that life has not yet entered.

"Rico asked me: What are you doing with St. Mawr? When I said we were taking him with us, he said: 'Oh, the *corpus delicti!*' Whether that means anything, I don't know. But he has grown sarcastic beyond my depth.

"I shall see you to-morrow--"

Lou arrived in town, at the dead end of August, with her maid and Phoenix. How wonderful it seemed to have London empty of all her set: her own little house to herself, with just the housekeeper and her own maid. The fact of being alone in those surroundings was so wonderful. It made the surroundings themselves seem all the more ghastly. Everything that had been actual to her was turning ghostly: even her little drawing-room was the ghost of a room, belonging to the dead people who had known it, or to all the dead generations that had brought such a room into being, evolved it out of their quaint domestic desires. And now, in herself, those desires were suddenly spent: gone out like a lamp that suddenly dies. And then she saw her pale, delicate room with its little green agate bowl and its two little porcelain birds and its soft, roundish chairs, turned into something ghostly, like a room set out in a museum. She felt like fastening little labels on the furniture: 'Lady Louise Carrington Lounge Chair, Last used August, 1923: Not for the benefit of posterity: but to remove her own self into another world, another realm of existence.

"My house, my house, my house, how can I ever have taken so much pains about it?" she kept saying to herself. It was like one of her old hats, suddenly discovered neatly put away in an old hat-box. And what a horror: an old 'fashionable' hat.

Lewis came to see her, and he sat there in one of her delicate mauve chairs, with his feet on a delicate old carpet from Turkestan, and she just wondered. He wore his leather gaiters and khaki breeches as usual, and a faded blue shirt. But his beard and hair were trimmed, he was tidy. There was a certain fineness of contour about him, a certain subtle gleam, which made him seem, apart from his rough boots, not at all gross, or coarse, in that setting of rather silky, Oriental furnishings. Rather he made the Asiatic, sensuous exquisiteness of her old rugs and her old white Chinese figures seem a weariness. Beauty! What was beauty? she asked herself. The Oriental exquisiteness seemed to her all like dead flowers whose hour had come to be thrown away.

Lou could understand her mother's wanting, for a moment, to marry him. His detachedness and his acceptance of something in destiny which people cannot accept. Right in the middle of him he accepted something from destiny that gave him a quality of eternity. He did not care about persons, people, even events. In his own odd way he was an aristocrat, inaccessible in his aristocracy. But it was the aristocracy of the invisible powers, the greater influences, nothing to do with human society.

"You don't really want to leave St. Mawr, do you?" Lou asked him. "You don't really want to quit, as you said?"

He looked at her steadily from his pale grey eyes, without answering, not knowing what to say.

"Mother told me what she said to you.--But she doesn't mind, she says you are entirely within your rights. She has a real regard for you. But we mustn't let our regards run us into actions which are beyond our scope, must we? That makes everything unreal. But you will come with us to America with St. Mawr, won't you? We depend on you."

"I don't want to be uncomfortable," he said.

"Don't be," she smiled. "I myself hate unreal situations--I feel I can't stand them any more. And most marriages are unreal situations. But apart from anything exaggerated, you like being with mother and me, don't you?"

"Yes, I do. I like Mrs. Witt as well. But not--"

"I know. There won't be any more of that--"

"You see, Lady Carrington", he said, with a little heat, "I'm not by nature a marrying man. And I'd feel I was selling myself."

"Quite!--Why do you think you are not a marrying man, though?"

"Me! I don't feel myself after I've been with women." He spoke in a low tone, looking down at his hands. "I feel messed up. I'm better to keep to myself.--Because--" and here he looked up with a flare in his eyes: "women--they only want to make you give in to them, so that they feel almighty, and you feel small."

"Don't you like feeling small?" Lou smiled. "And don't you want to make them give in to you?"

"Not me," he said. "I don't want nothing. Nothing, I want."

"Poor mother!" said Lou. "She thinks if she feels moved by a man, it must result in marriage--or that kind of thing. Surely she makes a mistake. I think you and Phoenix and mother and I might live somewhere in a far-away wild place, and make a good life: so long as we didn't begin to mix up marriage, or love or that sort of thing into it. It seems to me men and women have really hurt one another so much nowadays that they had better stay apart till they have learned to be gentle with one another again. Not all this forced passion and destructive philandering. Men and women should stay apart till their hearts grow gentle towards one another again. Now, it's only each one fighting for his own--or her own--underneath the cover of tenderness."

"*Dear!--darling!--Yes, my love!*" mocked Lewis, with a faint smile of amused contempt.

"Exactly. People always say *dearest!* when they hate each other most."

Lewis nodded, looking at her with a sudden sombre gloom in his eyes. A queer bitterness showed on his mouth. But even then he was so still and remote.

The housekeeper came and announced The Honourable Laura Ridley. This was like a blow in the face to Lou. She rose hurriedly--and Lewis rose, moving to the door.

"Don't go, please, Lewis," said Lou--and then Laura Ridley appeared in the doorway. She was a woman a few years older than Lou, but she looked younger. She might have been a shy girl of twenty-two, with her fresh complexion, her hesitant manner, her round, startled brown eyes, her bobbed hair.

"Hello!" said the newcomer. "Imagine your being back! I saw you in Paddington."

Those sharp eyes would see everything.

"I thought everyone was out of town," said Lou. "This is Mr. Lewis."

Laura gave him a little nod, then sat on the edge of her chair.

"No," she said. "I did go to Ireland to my people, but I came back. I prefer London when I can be more or less alone in it. I thought I'd just run in for a moment before you're gone again.--Scotland, isn't it?"

"No, mother and I are going to America."

"America! Oh, I thought it was Scotland."

"It was. But we have suddenly to go to America."

"I see!--And what about Rico?"

"He is staying on in Shropshire. Didn't you hear of his accident?"

Lou told about it briefly.

"But how awful!" said Laura. "But there! I knew it! I had a premonition when I saw that 'horse. We had a horse that killed a man. Then my father got rid of it. But ours was a mare, that one. Yours is a boy."

"A full-grown man, I'm afraid."

"Yes, of course, I remember.--But how awful! I suppose you won't ride in the Row. The awful people that ride there nowadays, anyhow! Oh, aren't they awful! Aren't people monstrous, really! My word, when I see the horses crossing Hyde Park Corner on a wet day and coming down smash to those slippery stones, giving their riders a fractured skull!--No joke!"

She inquired details of Rico.

"Oh, I suppose I shall see him when he gets back," she said. "But I'm sorry you are going. I shall miss you, I'm afraid. Though you won't be staying long in America. No one stays there longer than they can help."

"I think the winter through, at least," said Lou.

"Oh, all the winter! So long? I'm sorry to hear *that*. You're one of the few, very few people one can talk *really* simply with. Extraordinary, isn't it, how few really simple people there are! And they get fewer and fewer. I stayed a fortnight with my people, and a week of that I was in bed. It was really horrible. They really try to take the life out of me, *really!* Just because one won't be as they are, and play their game. I simply refused, and came away."

"But you can't cut yourself off altogether," said Lou.

"No, I suppose not. One has to see somebody. Luckily one has a few artists for friends. They're the only real people, anyhow--" She glanced round inquisitively at Lewis, and said with a slight, impertinent, elvish smile on her virgin face:

"Are you an artist?"

"No, Mam!" he said. "I'm a groom."

"Oh, I see!" She looked him up and down.

"Lewis is St. Mawr's master," said Lou.

"Oh, the horse! the terrible horse!" She paused a moment. Then again she turned to Lewis with that faint smile, slightly condescending, slightly impertinent, slightly flirtatious.

"Aren't you afraid of him?" she asked.

"No, Mam."

"Aren't you, *really*!--And can you always master him?"

"Mostly. He knows me."

"Yes! I suppose that's it."--She looked him up and down again, then turned away to Lou.

"What have you been painting lately?" said Lou. Laura was not a bad painter.

"Oh, hardly anything. I haven't been able to get on at all. This is one of my bad intervals."

Here Lewis rose and looked at Lou.

"All right," she said. "Come in after lunch, and we'll finish those arrangements."

Laura gazed after the man, as he dived out of the room, as if her eyes were gimlets that could bore into his secret. In the course of the conversation she said:

"What a curious little man that was!"

"Which?"

"The groom who was here just now. Very curious! Such peculiar eyes. I shouldn't wonder if he had psychic powers."

"What sort of psychic powers?" said Lou.

"Could see things.--And hypnotic, too. He might have hypnotic powers."

"What makes you think so?"

"He gives me that sort of feeling. Very curious! Probably he hypnotises the horse.--Are you leaving the horse here, by the way, in stable?"

"No, taking him to America."

"Taking him to America! How extraordinary!"

"It's mother's idea. She thinks he might be valuable as a stock horse on a ranch. You know we still have interest in a ranch in Texas."

"Oh, I see! Yes, probably he'd be very valuable to improve the breed of the horses over there.--My father has some very lovely hunters. Isn't it disgraceful, he would never let me ride!"

"Why?"

"Because we girls weren't important, in his opinion.--So you're taking the horse to America! With the little man?"

"Yes, St. Mawr will hardly behave without him."

"I see--I see--ee--ee! Just you and Mrs. Witt and the little man. I'm sure you'll find he has psychic powers."

"I'm afraid I'm not so good at finding things out," said Lou.

"Aren't you? No, I suppose not. I am: I have a flair. I sort of *smell* things. Then the horse is already here, is he? When do you think you'll sail?"

"Mother is finding a merchant boat that will go to Galveston, Texas, and take us along with the horse. She knows people who will find the right thing. But it takes time."

"What a much nicer way to travel than on one of those great liners! Oh, how awful they are! So vulgar! Floating palaces they call them! My word, the people inside the palaces!--Yes, I should say that would be a much pleasanter way of travelling: on a cargo boat."

Laura wanted to go down to the Mews to see St. Mawr. The two women went together.

St. Mawr stood in his box, bright and tense as usual.

"Yes!" said Laura Ridley, with a slight hiss. "Yes! Isn't he beautiful. Such very perfect legs!"--She eyed him round with those gimlet, sharp eyes of hers. "Almost a pity to let him go out of England. We need some of his perfect bone, I feel.--But his eye. Hasn't he got a look in it, my word!"

"I can never see that he looks wicked," said Lou.

"Can't you!"--Laura had a slight hiss in her speech, a sort of aristocratic decision in her enunciation, that got on Lou's nerves.--"He looks wicked to me!"

"He's not *mean*," said Lou. "He'd never do anything mean to you."

"Oh, mean! I dare say not. No! I'll grant him that, he gives fair warning. His eye says *Beware*!--But isn't he a beauty, *isn't* he!" Lou could feel the peculiar reverence for St. Mawr's breeding, his show qualities. Herself, all she cared about was the horse himself, his real nature. "Isn't it extraordinary," Laura continued, "that you never get a *really* perfectly satisfactory animal! There's always something wrong. And in men too. Isn't it curious? there's always something--something wrong--or something missing. Why is it?"

"I don't know," said Lou. She felt unable to cope with any more. And she was glad when Laura left her.

The days passed slowly, quietly, London almost empty of Lou's acquaintances. Mrs. Witt was busy getting all sorts of papers and permits: such a fuss! The battle light was still in her eye. But about her nose was a dusky, pinched look that made Lou wonder.

Both women wanted to be gone: they felt they had already flown in spirit, and it was weary, having the body left behind.

At last all was ready: they only awaited the telegram to say when their cargo-boat would sail. Trunks stood there packed, like great stones locked for ever. The Westminster house seemed already a shell. Rico wrote and telegraphed tenderly, but there was a sense of relentless effort in it all, rather than of any tenderness. He had taken his position.

Then the telegram came, the boat was ready to sail.

"There, now!" said Mrs. Witt, as if it had been a sentence of death.

"Why do you look like that, mother?"

"I feel I haven't an ounce of energy left in my body."

"But how queer, for you, mother. Do you think you are ill?"

"No, Louise. I just feel that way: as if I hadn't an ounce of energy left in my body."

"You'll feel yourself again, once you are away."

"Maybe I shall."

After all, it was only a matter of telephoning. The hotel and the railway porters and taxi-men would do the rest.

It was a grey, cloudy day, cold even. Mother and daughter sat in a cold first-class carriage and watched the little Hampshire country-side go past: little, old, unreal it seemed to them both, and passing away like a dream whose edges only are in consciousness. Autumn! Was this autumn? Were these trees, fields, villages? It seemed but the dim, dissolved edges of a dream, without inward substance.

At Southampton it was raining: and just a chaos, till they stepped on to a clean boat, and were received by a clean young captain, quite sympathetic, and quite a gentleman. Mrs. Witt, however, hardly looked at him, but went down to her cabin and lay down in her bunk.

There, lying concealed, she felt the engines start, she knew the voyage had begun. But she lay still. She saw the clouds and the rain, and refused to be disturbed.

Lou had lunch with the young captain, and she felt she ought to be flirty. The young man was so polite and attentive. And she wished so much she were alone.

Afterwards, she sat on deck and saw the Isle of Wight pass shadowy, in a misty rain. She didn't know it was the Isle of Wight. To her, it was just the lowest bit of the British Isles. She saw it fading away: and with it, her life, going like a clot of shadow in a mist of nothingness. She had no feelings about it, none: neither about Rico, nor her London house, nor anything. All passing in a grey curtain of rainy drizzle, like a death, and she, with not a feeling left.

They entered the Channel, and felt the slow heave of the sea. And soon the clouds broke in a little wind. The sky began to clear. By mid-afternoon it was blue summer, on the blue, running waters of the Channel. And soon, the ship steering for Santander, there was the coast of France, the rocks twinkling like some magic world.

The magic world! And back of it, that post-war Paris, which Lou knew only too well, and which depressed her so thoroughly. Or that post-war Monte Carlo, the Riviera still more depressing even than Paris. No, no one must land, even on magic coasts. Else you found yourself in a railway station and a centre of civilisation in five minutes.

Mrs. Witt hated the sea, and stayed, as a rule, practically the whole time' of the crossing in her bunk. There she was now, silent, shut up like a steel trap, as in her tomb. She did not even read. Just lay and stared at the passing sky. And the only thing to do was to leave her alone.

Lewis and Phoenix hung on the rail and watched everything. Or they went down to see St. Mawr. Or they stood talking in the doorway of the wireless operator's cabin. Lou begged the captain to give them jobs to do.

The queer, transitory, unreal feeling, as the ship crossed the great, heavy Atlantic. It was rather bad weather. And Lou felt, as she had felt before, that this grey, wolf-like, cold-blooded ocean hated men and their ships and their smoky passage. Heavy grey waves, a low-sagging sky: rain: yellow, weird evenings with snatches of sun: so it went on. Till they got way south, into the westward-running stream. Then they began to get blue weather and blue water.

To go south! Always to go south, away from the Arctic horror as far as possible! That was Lou's instinct. To go out of the clutch of greyness and low skies, of sweeping rain, and of slow, blanketing snow. Never again to see the mud and rain and snow of a northern winter, nor to feel the idealistic, Christianised tension of the now irreligious North.

As they neared Havana, and the water sparkled at night with phosphorus, and the flying-fishes came like drops of bright water, sailing out of the massive-slippery waves, Mrs. Witt emerged once more. She still had that shut-up, deathly look on her face. But she prowled round the deck, and manifested at least a little interest in affairs not her own. Here at sea she hardly remembered the existence of St. Mawr or Lewis or Phoenix. She was not very deeply aware even of Lou's existence.--But, of course, it would all come back, once they were on land.

They sailed in hot sunshine out of a blue, blue sea, past the castle into the harbour of Havana. There was a lot of shipping: and this was already America. Mrs. Witt had herself and Lou put ashore immediately. They took a motor-car and drove at once to the great boulevard that is the centre of Havana. Here they saw a long rank of motor-cars, all drawn up ready to take a couple of hundred American tourists for one more tour. There were the tourists, all with badges in their coats, lest they should get lost.

"They get so drunk by night," said the driver in Spanish, "that the policemen find them lying in the road--turn them over, see the badge--and, hup!--carry them to their hotel." He grinned sardonically.

Lou and her mother lunched at the Hotel d'Angleterre, and Mrs. Witt watched transfixed while a couple of her countrymen, a stout successful man and his wife, lunched abroad. They had cocktails--then lobster--and a bottle of hock--then a bottle of champagne--then a half-bottle of port.--And Mrs. Witt rose in haste as the liqueurs came. For that successful man and his wife had gone on imbibing with a sort of fixed and deliberate will, apparently tasting nothing, but saying to themselves: Now we're drinking Rhine wine! Now we're drinking 1912 champagne. Yah, Prohibition! Thou canst not put it over me.--Their complexions became more and more lurid. Mrs. Witt fled, fearing a Havana *débâcle*. But she said nothing.

In the afternoon, they motored into the country to see the great brewery gardens, the new villa suburb, and through the lanes past the old, decaying plantations with palm trees. In one lane they met the fifty motor-cars with the two hundred tourists all with badges on their chests and self-satisfaction on their faces. Mrs. Witt watched in grim silence.

"Plus ça change, plus c'est la même chose," said Lou, with a wicked little smile. *"On n'est pas mieux ici,* mother."

"I know it," said Mrs. Witt.

The hotels by the sea were all shut up: it was not yet the 'y 'season'. Not till November. And then I--Why, then Havana would be an American city, in full leaf of green dollar The green leaf of American prosperity shedding itself recklessly, from every roaming sprig of a tourist, over this city of sunshine and alcohol. Green leaves unfolded in Pittsburg and Chicago, showering in winter downfall in Havana.

Mother and daughter drank tea in a corner of the Mel d'Angleterre once more, and returned to the ferry.

The Gulf of Mexico was blue and rippling, with the phantom of islands on the south. Great porpoises rolled and leaped, running in front of the ship in the clear water, diving, travelling in perfect motion, straight, with the tip of the ship touching the tip of their tails, then rolling over, corkscrewing, and showing their bellies as they went. Marvellous! The marvellous beauty and fascination of natural wild things! The horror of man's unnatural life, his heaped-up civilisation! The flying fishes burst out of the sea in clouds of silvery, transparent motion. Blue above and below, the Gulf seemed a silent, empty, timeless place where man did not really reach. And Lou was again fascinated by the glamour of the universe. But bump! She and her mother were in a first-class hotel again, calling down the telephone for the bell-boy and iced water. And soon they were in a Pullman, off towards San Antonio.

It was America, it was Texas. They were at their ranch, on the great level of yellow autumn, with the vast sky above. And after all, from the hot, wide sky, and the hot, wide, red earth, there *did* come something new, something not used up. Lou did feel exhilarated.

The Texans were there, tall, blond people, ingenuously cheerful, ingenuously, childishly intimate, as if the fact that you had never seen them before was as nothing compared to the fact that you'd all been living in one room together all your lives, so that nothing was hidden from either of you. The one room being the mere shanty of the world in which we all live. Strange, uninspired cheerfulness, filling, as it were, the blank of complete incomprehension.

And off they set in their motor-cars, chiefly high-legged Fords, rattling away down the red trails between yellow sunflowers or sere grass or dry cotton, away, away into great distances, cheerfully raising the dust of haste. It left Lou in a sort of blank amazement. But it left her amused, not depressed. The old screws of emotion and intimacy that had been screwed down so tightly upon her fell out of their holes here. The Texan intimacy weighed no more on her than a postage stamp, even if, for the moment, it stuck as close. And there was a certain underneath recklessness, even a stoicism In all the apparently childish people, which left one free. They might appear childish: but they stoically depended on themselves alone, in reality. Not as in England, where every man waited to pour the burden of himself upon you.

St. Mawr arrived safely, a bit bewildered. The Texans eyed him closely, struck silent, as ever, by anything pure-bred and beautiful. He was somehow too beautiful, too perfected, in this great open country. The long-legged Texan horses, with their elaborate saddles, seemed somehow more natural.

Even St. Mawr felt himself strange, as it were naked and singled out, in this rough place. Like a jewel among stones, a pearl before swine, maybe. But the swine were no fools. They knew a pearl from a grain of maize, and a grain of maize from a pearl. And they knew what they wanted. When it was pearls, it was pearls; though chiefly, it was maize. Which shows good sense. They could see St. Mawr's points. Only he needn't draw the point too fine or it would just not pierce the tough skin of this country.

The ranch-man mounted him--just threw a soft skin over his back, jumped on, and away down the red trail, raising the dust among the tall, wild, yellow of sunflowers, in the hot, wild sun. Then back again in a fume, and the man slipped off.

"He's got the stuff in him, he sure has," said the man.

And the horse seemed pleased with this rough handling. Lewis looked on in wonder, and a little envy.

Lou and her mother stayed a fortnight on the ranch. It was all so queer: so crude, so rough, so easy, so artificially civilised, and so meaningless. Lou could not get over the feeling that it all meant nothing. There were no roots of reality at all. No consciousness below the surface, no meaning in anything save the obvious, the blatantly obvious. It was like life enacted in a mirror. Visually, it was wildly vital. But there was nothing behind it. Or like a cinematograph: flat shapes, exactly like men, but without any substance of reality, rapidly rattling away with talk, emotions, activity, all in the flat, nothing behind it. No deeper consciousness at all. So it seemed to her.

One moved from dream to dream, from phantasm to phantasm.

But at least, this Texan life, if it had no bowels, no vitals, at least it could not prey on one's own vitals. It was this much better than Europe.

Lewis was silent, and rather piqued. St. Mawr had already made advances to the boss's long-legged, arched-necked glossy-maned Texan mare. And the boss was pleased.

What a world!

Mrs. Witt eyed it all shrewdly. But she failed to participate. Lou was a bit scared at the emptiness of it all, and the queer, phantasmal self-consciousness. Cowboys just as self-conscious as Rico, far more sentimental, inwardly vague and unreal. Cowboys that went after their cows in black Ford motorcars: and who self-consciously saw Lady Carrington falling to them, as elegant young ladies from the East fall to the noble cowboy of the films, or in Zane Grey. It was all film-psychology.

And at the same time, these boys led a hard, hard life, often dangerous and gruesome. Nevertheless, inwardly they were self-conscious film heroes. The boss himself, a man over forty, long and lean and with a great deal of stringy energy, showed off before her in a strong silent manner, existing for the time being purely in his imagination of the sort of picture he made to her, the sort of impression he made on her.

So they all were, coloured up like a Zane Grey book-jacket, all of them living in the mirror. The kind of picture they made to somebody else.

And at the same time, with energy, courage, and a stoical grit getting their work done, and putting through what they had to put through.

It left Lou blank with wonder. And in the face of this strange, cheerful living in the mirror--a rather cheap mirror at that--England began to seem real to her again.

Then she had to remember herself back in England. And no, oh God, England was not real either, except poisonously. What was real? What under heaven was real?

Her mother had gone dumb and, as it were, out of range. Phoenix was a bit assured and bouncy, back more or less in his own conditions. Lewis was a bit impressed by the emptiness of everything, the lack of concentration. And St. Mawr followed at the heels of the boss's long-legged black Texan mare, almost slavishly.

What, in heaven's name, was one to make of it all?

Soon, she could not stand this sort of living in a film-setting, with the mechanical energy of 'making good', that is, making money, to keep the show going. The mystic duty to 'make good', meaning to make the ranch pay a laudable interest on the 'owners'' investment. Lou herself being one of the owners. And the interest that came to her, from her father's will, being the money she spent to buy St. Mawr and to fit up that house in Westminster. Then also the mystic duty to 'feel good'. Everybody had to *feel good, fine*! "How are you this morning, Mr. Latham?"--"*Fine*! Eh! Don't you feel good out here, eh? Lady Carrington?"--"*Fine!*"--Lou pronounced it with the same ringing conviction. It was Coué all the time!

"Shall we stay here long, mother?" she asked.

"Not a day longer than you want to, Louise. I stay entirely for your sake."

"Then let us go, mother."

They left St. Mawr and Lewis. But Phoenix wanted to come along. So they motored to San Antonio, got into the Pullman, and travelled as far as El Paso. Then they changed to go North. Santa Fe would be at least 'easy'. And Mrs. Witt had acquaintances there.

They found the fiesta over in Santa Fe: Indians, Mexicans, artists had finished their great effort to amuse and attract the tourists. "Welcome, Mr. Tourist" said a great board on one side of the high-road. And on the other side, a little nearer to town: "Thank You, Mr. Tourist."

"*Plus ça change--*" Lou began.

"*Ça ne change jamais*--except for the worse!" said Mrs. Witt, like a pistol going off. And Lou held her peace, after she had sighed to herself, and said in her own mind: 'Welcome Also, Mrs. and Miss Tourist!'

There was no getting a word out of Mrs. Witt these days. Whereas Phoenix was becoming almost loquacious.

They stayed a while in Santa Fé, in the clean, comfortable, 'homely' hotel, where 'every room had its bath': a spotless white bath, with very hot water night and day. The tourists and commercial travellers sat in the big hall down below, everybody living in the mirror! And of course, they knew Lady Carrington down to her shoe-soles. And they all expected her to know them down to their shoe-soles. For the only object of the mirror is to reflect images.

For two days mother and daughter ate in the mayonnaise intimacy of the dining-room. Then Mrs.. Witt struck, and telephoned down every meal-time for her meal in her room. She got to staying in bed later and later, as on the ship. Lou became uneasy. This was worse than Europe.

Phoenix was still there, as a sort of half-friend, half-servant retainer. He was perfectly happy, roving round among the Mexicans and Indians, talking Spanish all day, and telling about England and his two mistresses, rolling the ball of his own importance.

"I'm afraid we've got Phoenix for life," said Lou.

"Not unless we wish," said Mrs. Witt indifferently. And she picked up a novel which she didn't want to read, but which she was going to read.

"What shall we do next, mother?" Lou asked.

"As far as I am concerned, there is no next," said Mrs. Witt. "Come, mother! Let's go back to Italy or somewhere, if it's as bad as that."

"Never again, Louise, shall I cross that water. I have come home to die."

"I don't see much home about it--the Gonsalez Hotel in Santa Fe."

"Indeed not! But as good as anywhere else to die in."

"Oh, mother, don't be silly! Shall we look for somewhere where we can be by ourselves?"

"I leave it to you, Louise. I have made my last decision."

"What is that, mother?"

"Never, never to make another decision!"

"Not even to decide to die?"

"No, not even that."

"Or not to die?"

"Not that either."

Mrs. Witt shut up like a trap. She refused to rise from her bed that day.

Lou went to consult Phoenix. The result was, the two set out to look at a little ranch that was for sale.

It was autumn, and the loveliest time in the south-west, where there is no spring, snow blowing into the hot lap of summer; and no real summer, hail falling in thick ice from the thunderstorms: and even no very definite winter, hot sun melting the snow and giving an impression of spring at any time. But autumn there is, when the winds of the desert are almost still, and the mountains fume no clouds. But morning comes cold and delicate, upon the wild sunflowers and the puffing, yellow-flowered greasewood. For the desert blooms in autumn. In spring it is grey ash all the time, and only the strong breath of the summer sun, and the heavy splashing of thunder rain succeeds at last, by September, in blowing it into soft puffy yellow fire.

It was such a delicate morning when Lou drove out with Phoenix towards the mountains, to look at this ranch that a Mexican wanted to sell. For the brief moment the high mountains had lost their snow: it would be back again in a fortnight: and stood dim and delicate with autumn haze. The desert stretched away pale, as pale as the sky, but silvery and sere, with hummock-mounds of shadow, and long wings of shadow, like the reflection of some great bird. The same eagle shadows came like rude paintings of the outstretched bird, upon the mountains, where the aspens were turning yellow. For the moment, the brief moment, the great desert-and-mountain landscape had lost its certain cruelty, and looked tender, dreamy. And many, many birds were flickering around.

Lou and Phoenix bumped and hesitated over a long trail: then wound down into a deep canyon: and then the car began to climb, climb, climb, in steep rushes, and in long, heartbreaking, uneven pulls. The road was bad, and driving was no joke. But it was the sort of road Phoenix was used to. He sat impassive and watchful, and kept on, till his engine boiled. He was *himself* in this country: impassive, detached, self-satisfied, and silently assertive. Guarding himself at every moment, but, on his guard, sure of himself. Seeing no difference at all between Lou or Mrs. Witt and himself, except that they had money and he had none, while he had a native importance which they lacked. He depended on them for money, they on him for the power to live out here in the West. Intimately, he was as good as they. Money was their only advantage.

As Lou sat beside him in the front seat of the car, where it bumped less than behind, she felt this. She felt a peculiar, tough-necked arrogance in him, as if he were asserting himself to put something over her. He wanted her to allow him to make advances to her, to allow him to suggest that he should be her lover. And then, finally, she would marry him, and he would be on the same footing as she and her mother.

In return, he would look after her, and give her his support and countenance, as a man, and stand between her and the world. In this sense, he would be faithful to her, and loyal. But as far as other women went, Mexican women or Indian women: why, that was none of her business. His marrying her would be a pact between two aliens, on behalf of one another, and he would keep his part of it all right. But himself, as a private man and a predative alien-blooded male, this had nothing to do with her. It didn't enter into her scope and count. She was one of these nervous white women with lots of money. She was very nice, too. But as a squaw--as a real woman in a shawl whom a man went after for the pleasure of the night--why, she hardly counted. One of these white women who talk clever and know things like a man. She could hardly expect a half-savage male to acknowledge her as his female counterpart--No! She had the bucks! And she had all the paraphernalia of the white man's civilisation, which a savage can play with and so escape his own hollow boredom. But his own real female counterpart?--Phoenix would just have shrugged his shoulders, and thought the question not worth answering. How could there be any answer in her, to the phallic male in him? Couldn't! Yet it would flatter his vanity and his self-esteem immensely, to possess her. That would be possessing the very clue to the white man's overwhelming world. And if she would let him possess her, he would be absolutely loyal to her, as far as affairs and appearances went. Only, the aboriginal phallic male in him simply couldn't recognise her as a woman at all. In this respect, she didn't exist. It needed the shawled Indian or Mexican women, with their squeaky, plaintive voices, their shuffling, watery humility, and the dark glances of their big, knowing eyes. When an Indian woman looked at him from under her black fringe, with dark, half-secretive suggestion in her big eyes: and when she stood before him hugged in her shawl, in such apparently complete quiescent humility: and when she spoke to him in her mousey squeak of a high, plaintive voice, as if it were difficult for her female bashfulness even to emit so much sound: and when she shuffled away with her legs wide apart, because of her wide-topped, white, high buckskin boots with tiny white feet, and her dark-knotted hair so full of hard, yet subtle lure: and when he remembered the almost watery softness of the Indian woman's dark, warm flesh: then he was a male, an old, secretive, rat-like male. But before Lou's straightforwardness and utter sexual incompetence, he just stood in contempt. And to him, even a French cocotte was utterly devoid of the right sort of sex. She couldn't really move him. She couldn't satisfy the furtiveness in him. He needed this plaintive, squeaky, dark-fringed Indian quality, something furtive and soft and rat-like, really to rouse him.

Nevertheless, he was ready to trade his sex, which, in his opinion, every white woman was secretly pining for, for the white woman's money and social privileges. In the day-time, all the thrill and excitement of the white man's motor-cars and moving pictures and ice-cream sodas, and so forth. In the night, the soft, watery-soft warmth of an Indian or half-Indian woman. This was Phoenix's idea of life for himself.

Meanwhile, if a white woman gave him the privileges of the white man's world, he would do his duty by her as far as all that went.

Lou, sitting very, very still beside him as he drove the car--he was not a very good driver, not quick and marvellous as some white men are, particularly some French chauffeurs she had known, but usually a little behindhand in his movements--she knew more or less all that he felt. More or less she divined as a woman does. Even from a certain rather assured stupidity of his shoulders, and a certain rather stupid assertiveness of his knees, she knew him.

But she did not judge him too harshly. Somewhere deep, deep in herself she knew she too was at fault. And this made her sometimes inclined to humble herself, as a woman, before the furtive assertiveness of this underground, 'knowing' savage. He was so different from Rico.

Yet, after all, was he? In his rootlessness, his drifting, his real meaninglessness, was he different from Rico? And his childish, spellbound absorption in the motor-car, or in the moving pictures, or in an ice-cream soda--was it very different from Rico? Anyhow, was it really any better? Pleasanter, perhaps, to a woman, because of the childishness of it.

The same with his opinion of himself as a sexual male! So childish, really, it was almost thrilling to a woman. But then, so stupid also, with that furtive lurking in holes and imagining it could not be detected He imagined he kept himself dark, in his sexual rat-holes. He imagined he was not detected.

No, no, Lou was not such a fool as she looked, in his eyes, anyhow. She knew what she wanted. She wanted relief from the nervous tension and irritation of her life, she wanted to escape from the friction which is the whole stimulus in modern social life. She wanted to be still: only that, to be very, very still, and recover her own soul.

When Phoenix presumed she was looking for some secretly sexual male such as himself, he was ridiculously mistaken. Even the illusion of the beautiful St. Mawr was gone. And Phoenix, roaming round like a sexual rat in promiscuous back yards!--*Merci, mon cher*! For that was all he was: a sexual rat in the great barn-yard of man's habitat, looking for female rats!

Merci, mon cher! You are had.

Nevertheless, in his very mistakenness, he was a relief to her. His mistake was amusing rather than impressive. And the fact that one half of his intelligence was a complete dark blank, that too was a relief.

Strictly, and perhaps in the best sense, he was a servant. His very unconsciousness and his very limitation served as a shelter, as one shelters within the limitations of four walls. The very decided limits to his intelligence were a shelter to her. They made her feel safe.

But that feeling of safety did not deceive her. It was the feeling one derived from having a true servant attached to one, a man whose psychic limitations left him incapable of anything but service, and whose strong flow of natural life, at the same time, made him need to serve.

And Lou, sitting there so very still and frail, yet self-contained, had not lived for nothing. She no longer wanted to fool herself. She had no desire at all to fool herself into thinking that a Phoenix might be a husband and a mate. No desire that way at all. His obtuseness was a servant's obtuseness. She was grateful to him for serving, and she paid him a wage. Moreover, she provided him with something to do, to occupy his life. In a sense, she gave him his life, and rescued him from his own boredom. It was a balance.

He did not know what she was thinking. There was a certain physical sympathy between them. His obtuseness made him think it was also a sexual sympathy.

"It's a nice trip, you and me," he said suddenly, turning and looking her in the eyes with an excited look, and ending on a foolish little laugh.

She realised that she should have sat in the back seat.

"But it's a bad road," she said. "Hadn't you better stop and put the sides of the hood up? Your engine is boiling."

He looked away with a quick switch of interest to the red thermometer in front of his machine.

"She's boiling," he said, stopping, and getting out with a quick alacrity to go to look at the engine.

Lou got out also, and went to the back seat, shutting the door decisively.

"I think I'll ride at the back," she said, "it gets so frightfully hot in front when the engine heats up.--Do you think she needs some water? Have you got some in the canteen?"

"She's full," he said, peering into the steaming valve.

"You can run a bit out, if you think there's any need. I wonder if it's much farther!"

"*Quién sabe!*" said he, slightly impertinent.

She relapsed into her own stillness. She realised how careful, how very careful she must be of relaxing into sympathy, and reposing, as it were, on Phoenix. He would read it as a sexual appeal. Perhaps he couldn't help it. She had only herself to blame. He was obtuse, as a man and a savage. He had only one interpretation, sex, for any woman's approach to him.

And she knew, with the last clear knowledge of weary disillusion, that she did not want to be mixed up in Phoenix's sexual promiscuities. The very thought was an insult to her. The crude, clumsy servant-male: no, no, not that. He was a good fellow, a very good fellow, as far as he went. But he fell far short of physical intimacy.

"No, no," she said to herself, "I was wrong to ride in the front seat with him. I must sit alone, just alone. Because sex, mere sex, is repellent to me. I will never prostitute myself again. Unless something touches my very spirit, the very quick of me, I will stay alone, just alone. Alone, and give myself only to the unseen presences, serve only the other, unseen presences."

She understood now the meaning of the Vestal Virgins, the Virgins of the holy fire in the old temples. They were symbolic of herself, of woman weary of the embrace of incompetent men, weary, weary, weary of all that, turning to the unseen gods, the unseen spirits, the hidden fire, and devoting herself to that, and that alone. Receiving thence her pacification and her fulfilment.

Not these little, incompetent, childish self-opinionated men! Not these to touch her. She watched Phoenix's rather stupid shoulders as he drove the car on between the piñon trees and the cedars of the narrow mesa ridge, to the mountain foot. He was a good fellow. But let him run among women of his own sort. Something was beyond him. And this something must remain beyond him, never allow itself to come within his reach. Otherwise he would paw it and mess it up, and be as miserable as a child that has broken its father's watch.

No, no! She had loved an American, and lived with him for a fortnight. She had had a long, intimate friendship with an Italian. Perhaps it was love on his part. And she had yielded to him. Then her love and marriage to Rico.

And what of it all? Nothing. It was almost nothing. It was as if only the outside of herself, her top layers, were human. This inveigled her into intimacies. As soon as the intimacy penetrated, or attempted to penetrate, inside her, it was a disaster. Just a humiliation and a breaking down.

Within these outer layers of herself lay the successive inner sanctuaries of herself. And these were inviolable. She accepted it.

"I am not a marrying woman," she said to herself. "I'm not a lover nor a mistress nor a wife. It is no good. Love can't really come into me from the outside, and I can never, never mate with any man, since the mystic new man will never come to me. No, no, let me know myself and my role. I am one of the eternal Virgins, serving the eternal fire. My dealings with men have only broken my stillness and messed up my doorways. It has been my own fault. I ought to stay virgin, and still, very, very still, and serve the most perfect service. I want my temple and my loneliness and my Apollo mystery of the inner fire. And with men, only the delicate, subtler, more remote relations. No coming near. A coming near only breaks the delicate veils, and broken veils, like broken flowers, only lead to rottenness."

She felt a great peace inside herself as she made this realisation. And a thankfulness. Because, after all, it seemed to her that the hidden fire was alive and burning in this sky, over the desert, in the mountains. She felt a certain latent holiness in the very atmosphere, a young, spring-fire of latent holiness, such as she had never felt in Europe or in the East. "For me," she said, as she looked away at the mountains in shadow and the pale, warm desert beneath, with wings of shadow upon it: "For me, this place is sacred. It is blessed."

But as she watched Phoenix: as she remembered the motorcars and tourists, and the rather dreary Mexicans of Santa Fe, and the lurking, invidious Indians, with something of a rat-like secretiveness and defeatedness in their bearing, she realised that the latent fire of the vast landscape struggled under a great weight of dirt-like inertia. She had to mind the dirt, most carefully and vividly avoid it and keep it away from her, here in this place that at last seemed sacred to her.

The motor-car climbed up, past the tall pine trees, to the foot of the mountains, and came at last to a wire gate, where nothing was to be expected. Phoenix opened the gate, and they drove on, through more trees, into a clearing where dried-up bean plants were yellow.

"This man got no water for his beans," said Phoenix. "Not got much beans this year."

They climbed slowly up the incline, through more pine trees, and out into another clearing, where a couple of horses were grazing. And there they saw the ranch itself, little low cabins with patched roofs, under a few pine trees, and facing the long twelve-acre clearing, or field, where the Michaelmas daisies were purple mist, and spangled with clumps of yellow flowers.

"Not got no alfalfa here neither!" said Phoenix, as the car waded past the flowers. "Must be a dry place up here. Got no water, sure they haven't."

Yet it was the place Lou wanted. In an instant, her heart sprang to it. The instant the car stopped, and she saw the two cabins inside the rickety fence, the rather broken corral beyond, and behind all, tall, blue balsam pines, the round hills, the solid up-rise of the mountain flank: and getting down, she looked across the purple and gold of the clearing, downwards at the ring of pine trees standing so still, so crude and untameable, the motionless desert beyond the bristles of the pine crests, a thousand feet below: and beyond the desert, blue mountains, and far, far-off blue mountains in Arizona: "This is the place," she said to herself.

This little tumbledown ranch, only a homestead of a hundred and sixty acres, was, as it were, man's last effort towards the wild heart of the Rockies, at this point. Sixty years before, a restless schoolmaster had wandered out from the East, looking for gold among the mountains. He found a very little, then no more. But the mountains had got hold of him, he could not go back.

There was a little trickling spring of pure water, a thread of treasure perhaps better than gold. So the schoolmaster took up a homestead on the lot where this little spring arose. He struggled, and got himself his log cabin erected, his fence put up, sloping at the mountain-side through the pine trees and dropping into the hollows where the ghost-white mariposa lilies stood leafless and naked in flower, in spring, on tall, invisible stems. He made the long clearing for alfalfa.

And fell so into debt that he had to trade his homestead away, to clear his debt. Then he made a tiny living teaching the children of the few American prospectors who had squatted in the valleys, beside the Mexicans.

The trader who got the ranch tackled it with a will. He built another log cabin and a big corral, and brought water from the canyon two miles and more across the mountain slope, in a little runnel ditch, and more water, piped a mile or more down the little canyon immediately above the cabins. He got a flow of water for his houses: for being a true American, he felt he could not really say he had conquered his environment till he had got running water, taps, and wash-hand basins inside his house.

Taps, running water and wash-hand basins he accomplished. And, undaunted through the years, he prepared the basin for a fountain in the little fenced-in enclosure, and he built a little bath-house. After a number of years, he sent up the enamelled bath-tub to be put in the little log bath-house on the little wild ranch hung right against the savage Rockies, above the desert.

But here the mountains finished him. He was a trader down below, in the Mexican village. This little ranch was, as it were, his hobby, his ideal. He and his New England wife spent their summers there: and turned on the taps in the cabins and turned them off again, and felt really that civilisation had conquered.

All this plumbing from the savage ravines of the canyons--. one of them nameless to this day--cost, however, money. In fact, the ranch cost a great deal of money. But it was all to be got back. The big clearing was to be irrigated for alfalfa, the little clearing for beans, and the third clearing, under the corral, for potatoes. All these things the trader could trade to the Mexicans, very advantageously.

And, moreover, since somebody had started a praise of the famous goats' cheese made by Mexican peasants in New Mexico, goats there should be.

Goats there were: five hundred of them, eventually. And they fed chiefly in the wild mountain hollows, the no-man's-land. The Mexicans call them fire-mouths, because everything they nibble dies. Not because of their flaming mouths, really, but because they nibble a live plant down, down to the quick, till it can put forth no more.

So, the energetic trader, in the course of five or six years, had got the ranch ready. The long three-roomed cabin was for him and his New England wife. In the two-roomed cabin lived the Mexican family who really had charge of the ranch. For the trader was mostly fixed to his store, seventeen miles away, down in the Mexican village. /

The ranch lay over eight thousand feet up, the snows of winter came deep and the white goats, looking dirty yellow, swam in snow with their poor curved horns poking out like dead sticks. But the corral had a long, cosy, shut-in goat-shed all down one side, and into this crowded the five hundred, their acrid goat smell rising like hot acid over the snow. And the thin, pock-marked Mexican threw them alfalfa out of the log barn. Until the hot sun sank the snow again, and froze the surface, when patter-patter went the two thousand little goat-hoofs, over the silver-frozen snow, up at the mountain. Nibble, nibble, nibble, the fire-mouths, at every tender twig. And the goat-bell climbed, and the baa-ing came from among the dense and shaggy pine trees. And sometimes, in a soft drift under the trees, a goat, or several goats, went through, into the white depths, and some were lost thus, to reappear dead and frozen at the thaw.

By evening, they were driven down again, like a dirty yellowish-white stream carrying dark sticks on its yeasty surface, tripping and bleating over the frozen snow, past the bustling dark green pine trees, down to the trampled mess of the corral. And everywhere, everywhere over the snow, yellow stains and dark pills of goat-droppings melting into the surface crystal. On still, glittering nights, when the frost was hard, the smell of goats came up like some uncanny acid fire, and great stars sitting on the mountain's edge seemed to be watching like the eyes of a mountain lion, brought by the scent. Then the coyotes in the near canyon howled and sobbed, and ran like shadows over the snow. But the goat corral had been built tight.

In the course of years the goat-herd had grown from fifty to five hundred, and surely that was increase. The goat-milk cheeses sat drying on their little racks. In spring there was a great flowing and skipping of kids. In summer and early autumn, there was a pest of flies, rising from all that goat smell and that cast-out whey of goats' milk, after the cheese-making. The rats came, and the pack-rats, swarming.

And after all, it was difficult to sell or trade the cheeses, and little profit to be made. And in dry summers, no water came down in the narrow ditch-channel, that straddled in wooden runnels over the deep clefts in the mountain-side. No water meant no alfalfa. In winter the goats scarcely drank at all. In summer they could be watered at the little spring. But the thirsty land was not so easy to accommodate.

Five hundred fine white Angora goats, with their massive handsome padres! They were beautiful enough. And the trader made all he could of them. Come summer, they were run down into the narrow tank filled with the fiery dipping fluid. Then their lovely white wool was clipped. It was beautiful, and valuable, but comparatively little of it.

And it all cost, cost, cost. And a man was always let down. At one time no water. At another a poison weed. Then a sickness. Always some mysterious malevolence fighting, fighting against the will of man. A strange invisible influence coming out of the livid rock fastnesses in the bowels of those uncreated Rocky Mountains, preying upon the will of man, and slowly wearing down his resistance, his onward-pushing spirit. The curious, subtle thing, like a mountain fever, got into the blood, so that the men at the ranch, and the animals with them, had bursts of queer, violent, half-frenzied energy, in which, however, they were wont to lose their wariness. And then, damage of some sort. The horses ripped and cut themselves, or they were struck by lightning, the men had great hurts or sickness. A curious disintegration working all the time, a sort of malevolent breath, like a stupefying, irritant gas coming out of the unfathomed mountains.

The pack-rats with their bushy tails and big ears came down out of the hills, and were jumping and bouncing about: symbols of the curious debasing malevolence that was in the spirit of the place. The Mexicans in charge, good honest men, worked all they could. But they were like most of the Mexicans in the south-west, as if they had been pithed, to use one of Kipling's words. As if the invidious malevolence of the country itself had slowly taken all the pith of manhood from them, leaving a hopeless sort of corpus of a man.

And the same happened to the white men, exposed to the open country. Slowly, they were pithed. The energy went out of them. And more than that, the interest. An inertia of indifference invading the soul, leaving the body healthy and active, but wasting the soul, the living interest, quite away.

It was the New England wife of the trader who put most energy into the ranch. She looked on it as her home. She had a little white fence put all round the two cabins: the bright brass water-taps she kept shining in the two kitchens: outside the kitchen door she had a little kitchen garden and nasturtiums, after a great fight with invading animals, that nibbled everything away. And she got so far as the preparation of the round concrete basin which was to be a little pool, under the few enclosed pine trees between the two cabins, a pool with a tiny fountain jet.

But this, with the bath-tub, was her limit, as the five hundred goats were her man's limit. Out of the mountains came two breaths of influence: the breath of the curious, frenzied energy, that took away one's intelligence as alcohol or any other stimulus does: and then the most strange indiviousness that ate away the soul.

The woman loved her ranch, almost with passion. It was she who felt the stimulus more than the men. It seemed to enter her like a sort of sex passion, intensifying her ego, making her full of violence and of blind female energy. The energy and the blindness of it! A strange blind frenzy, like an intoxication while it lasted. And the sense of beauty that thrilled her New England woman's soul.

Her cabin faced the slow down-slope of the clearing, the alfalfa field: her long, low cabin, crouching under the great pine tree that threw up its trunk sheer in front of the house, in the yard. That pine tree was the guardian of the place. But a bristling, almost demonish guardian, from the far-off crude ages of the world. Its great pillar of pale, flakey-ribbed copper rose there in strange, callous indifference, and the grim permanence, which is in pine trees. A passionless, non-phallic column, rising in the shadows of the pre-sexual world, before the hot-blooded ithyphallic column ever erected itself. A cold, blossomless, resinous sap surging and oozing gum, from that pallid brownish bark. And the wind hissing in the needles, like a vast nest of serpents. And the pine cones falling plumb as the hail hit them. Then lying all over the yard, open in the sun like wooden roses, but hard, sexless, rigid with a blind will.

Past the column of that pine tree, the alfalfa field sloped gently down, to the circling guard of pine trees, from which silent, living barrier isolated pines rose to ragged heights at intervals, in blind assertiveness. Strange, those pine trees! In some lights all their needles glistened like polished steel, all subtly glittering with a whitish glitter among darkness, like real needles. Then again, at evening, the trunks would flare up orange red, and the tufts would be dark, alert tufts like a wolf's tail touching the air. Again, in the morning sunlight they would be soft and still, hardly noticeable. But all the same, present and watchful. Never sympathetic, always watchfully on their guard, and resistant, they hedged one in with the aroma and the power and the slight horror of the pre-sexual primeval world. The world where each creature was crudely limited to its own ego, crude and bristling and cold, and then crowding in packs like pine trees and wolves.

But beyond the pine trees, ah, there beyond, there was beauty for the spirit to soar in. The circle of pines, with the loose trees rising high and ragged at intervals, this was the barrier, the fence to the foreground. Beyond was only distance, the desert a thousand feet below, and beyond.

The desert swept its great fawn-coloured circle around, away beyond and below like a beach, with a long mountainside of pure blue shadow closing in the near corner, and strange, bluish hummocks of mountains rising like wet rock from a vast strand, away in the middle distance, and beyond, in the farthest distance, pale blue crests of mountains looking over the horizon from the west, as if peering in from another world altogether.

Ah, that was beauty!--perhaps the most beautiful thing in the world. It was pure beauty, *absolute* beauty! There! That was it. To the little woman from New England, with her tense, fierce soul and her egoistic passion of service, this beauty was absolute, a *ne plus ultra*. From her doorway, from her porch, she could watch the vast, eagle-like wheeling of the daylight, that turned as the eagles which lived in the near rocks turned overhead in the blue, turning their luminous, dark-edged-patterned bellies and underwings upon the pure air, like winged orbs. So the daylight made the vast turn upon the desert, brushing the farthest out-watching mountains. And sometimes the vast strand of the desert would float with curious undulations and exhalations amid the blue fragility of mountains, whose upper edges were harder than the floating bases. And sometimes she would see the little brown adobe houses of the village Mexicans, twenty miles away, like little cube crystals of insect-houses dotting upon the desert, very distinct, with a cotton-wood tree or two rising near. And sometimes she would see the far-off rocks thirty miles away, Where the canyon made a gateway between the mountains. Quite clear, like an open gateway out of the vast yard, she would see the cut-out bit of the canyon passage. And on the desert itself, curious, puckered folds of mesa-sides. And a blackish crack which in places revealed the otherwise invisible canyon of the Rio Grande. And beyond everything, the mountains like icebergs showing up from an outer sea. Then later, the sun would go down blazing above the shallow cauldron of simmering darkness, and the round mountains of Colorado would lump up into uncanny significance, northwards. That was always rather frightening. But morning came again, with the sun peeping over the mountain slopes and lighting the desert away in the distance long, long before it lighted on her yard. And then she would see another valley, like magic and very lovely, with green folds and long tufts of cotton-wood trees, and a few long-cubical adobe houses, lying float-ing in shallow light below, like a vision.

Ah! it was beauty, beauty absolute, at any hour of the day: whether the perfect clarity of morning or the mountains beyond the simmering desert at noon, or the purple lumping of northern mounds under a red sun at night. Or whether the dust whirled in tall columns, travelling across the desert far away, like pillars of cloud by day, tall, leaning pillars of dust hastening with ghostly haste: or whether, in the early part of the year, suddenly in the morning a whole sea of solid white would rise rolling below, a solid mist from melted snow, ghost-white under the mountain sun, the world below blotted out: or whether the black rain and cloud streaked down, far across the desert, and lightning stung down with sharp white stings on the horizon: or the cloud travelled and burst overhead, with rivers of fluid blue fire running out of heaven and exploding on earth, and hail coming down like a world of ice shattered above: or the hot sun rode in again: or snow fell in heavy silence: or the world was blinding white under a blue sky, and one must hurry under the pine trees for shelter against that vast, white, back-beating light which rushed up at one and made one almost unconscious, amid the snow.

It was always beauty, *always!* It was always great, and splendid, and, for some reason, natural. It was never grandiose or theatrical. Always, for some reason, per-fect. And quite simple, in spite of it all.

So it was, when you watched the vast and living landscape. The landscape lived, and lived as the world of the gods, unsullied and unconcerned. The great circling landscape lived its own life, sumptuous and uncaring. Man did not exist for it.

And if it had been a question simply of living through the eyes, into the distance, then this would have been Paradise, and the little New England woman on her ranch would have found what she was always looking for, the earthly paradise of the spirit.

But even a woman cannot live only into the distance, the beyond. Willy-nilly she finds herself juxtaposed to the near things, the thing in itself. And willy-nilly she is caught up into the fight with the immediate object.

The New England woman had fought to make the nearness as perfect as the distance: for the distance was absolute beauty. She had been confident of success. She had felt quite assured, when the water came running out of her bright brass taps, the wild water of the hills caught, tricked into the narrow iron pipes, and led tamely to her kitchen, to jump out over her sink, into her wash-basin, at her service. "There!" she said. "I have tamed the waters of the mountain to my service."

So she had, for the moment.

At the same time, the invisible attack was being made upon her. While she revelled in the beauty of the luminous world that wheeled around and below her, the grey, rat-like spirit of the inner mountains was attacking her from behind. She could not keep her attention. And, curiously, she could not keep even her speech. When she was saying something, suddenly the next word would be gone out of her, as if a pack-rat had carried it off. And she sat blank, stuttering, staring in the empty cupboard of her mind, like Mother Hubbard, and seeing the cupboard bare. And this irritated her husband intensely.

Her chickens, of which she was so proud, were carried away. Or they strayed. Or they fell sick. At first she could cope with their circumstances. But after a while, she couldn't. She couldn't care. A drug-like numbness possessed her spirit, and at the very middle of her, she couldn't care what happened to her chickens.

The same when a couple of horses were struck by lightning. It frightened her. The rivers of fluid fire that suddenly fell out of the sky and exploded on the earth nearby, as if the whole earth had burst like a bomb, frightened her from the very core of her, and made her know, secretly and with cynical certainty, that *there was no merciful God in the heavens*. A very tall, elegant pine tree just above her cabin took the lightning, and stood tall and elegant as before, but with a white seam spiralling from its crest, all down its tall trunk, to earth. The perfect scar, white and long as lightning itself. And every time she looked at it, she said to herself, in spite of herself: "There is no Almighty loving God. The God there is shaggy as the pine trees, and horrible as the lightning." Outwardly, she never confessed this. Openly, she thought of her dear New England Church as usual. But in the violent undercurrent of her woman's soul, after the storms, she would look at that living, seamed tree, and the voice would say in her, almost savagely: 'What nonsense about Jesus and a God of Love, in a place like this! This is more awful and more splendid. I like it better.' The very chipmunks, in their jerky helter-skelter, the blue jays wrangling in the pine tree in the dawn, the grey squirrel undulating to the tree-trunk, then pausing to chatter at her and scold her, with a shrewd fearlessness, as if she were the alien, the outsider, the creature that should not be permitted among the trees, all destroyed the illusion she cherished, of love, universal love. There was no love on this ranch. There was life, intense, bristling life, full of energy, but also, with an undertone of savage sordidness.

The black ants in her cupboard, the pack-rats bouncing on her ceiling like hippopotami in the night, the two sick goats: there was a peculiar undercurrent of squalor, flowing under the curious tussle of wild life. That was it. The wild life, even the life of the trees and flowers seemed one bristling, hair-raising tussle. The very flowers came up bristly, and many of them were fang-mouthed, like the dead-nettle: and none had any real scent. But they were very fascinating, too, in their very fierceness. In May, the curious columbines of the stream-beds, columbines scarlet outside and yellow in, like the red and yellow of a herald's uniform--farther from the dove nothing could be: then the beautiful rosy-blue of the great tufts of the flower they called bluebell, but which was really a flower of the snap-dragon family: these grew in powerful beauty in the little clearing of the pine trees, followed by the flower the settlers had mysteriously called herb honeysuckle: a tangle of long drops of pure fire-red, hanging from slim invisible stalks of smoke colour. The purest, most perfect vermilion scarlet, cleanest fire-colour, hanging in long drops like a shower of fire-rain that is just going to strike the earth. A little later, more in the open, there came another sheer fire-red flower, sparking, fierce red stars running up a bristly grey ladder, as if the earth's fire-centre had blown out some red sparks, white-speckled and deadly inside, puffing for a moment in the day air.

So it was! The alfalfa field was one raging, seething conflict of plants trying to get hold. One dry year, and the bristly wild things had got hold: the spiky, blue-leaved thistle-poppy with its moon-white flowers, the low clumps of blue nettle-flower, the later rush, after the sereneness of June and July, the rush of red sparks and Michaelmas daisies, and the tough, wild sunflowers, strangling and choking the dark, tender green of the clover-like alfalfa! A battle, a battle, with banners of bright scarlet and yellow.

When a really defenceless flower did issue, like the moth-still, ghost-centred mariposa lily, with its inner moth-dust of yellow, it came invisible. There was nothing to be seen but a hair of greyish grass near the oak scrub. Behold, this invisible long stalk was balancing a white, ghostly, three-petalled flower, naked out of nothingness. A mariposa lily!

Only the pink wild roses smelled sweet, like the old world. They were sweet-briar roses. And the dark blue harebells among the oak scrub, like the ice-dark bubbles of the mountain flowers in the Alps, the Alpenglocken.

The roses of the desert are the cactus flowers, crystal of translucent yellow or of rose-colour. But set among spines the devil himself must have conceived in a moment of sheer ecstasy.

Nay, it was a world before and after the God of Love. Even the very humming-birds hanging about the flowering squaw-berry bushes, when the snow had gone, in May, they were before and after the God of Love. And the blue jays were crested dark with challenge, and the yellow-and-dark woodpecker was fearless like a warrior in war-paint, as he struck the wood. While on the fence the hawks sat motionless, like dark fists clenched under heaven, ignoring man and his ways.

Summer, it was true, unfolded the tender cotton-wood leaves, and the tender aspen. But what a tangle and a ghostly aloofness in the aspen thickets high up on the mountains, the coldness that is in the eyes and the long cornelian talons of the bear.

Summer brought the little wild strawberries, with their savage aroma, and the late summer brought the rose-jewel raspberries in the valley cleft. But how lonely, how harsh-lonely and menacing it was, to be alone in that shadowy, steep cleft of a canyon just above the cabins, picking raspberries, while the thunder gathered thick and blue-purple at the mountain-tops. The many wild raspberries hanging rose-red in the thickets. But the stream bed below all silent, waterless. And the trees all bristling in silence, and waiting like warriors at an outpost. And the berries waiting for the sharp-eyed, cold, long-snouted bear to come rambling and shaking his heavy, sharp fur. The berries grew for the bears, and the little New England woman, with her uncanny sensitiveness to underlying influences, felt all the time she was stealing. Stealing the wild raspberries in the secret little canyon behind her home. And when she had made them into jam, she could almost taste the theft in her preserves.

She confessed nothing of this. She tried even to confess nothing of her dread. But she was afraid. Especially she was conscious of the prowling, intense aerial electricity all the summer, after June. The air was thick with wandering currents of fierce electric fluid, waiting to discharge themselves. And almost every day there was the rage and battle of thunder. But the air was never cleared. There was no relief. However, the thunder raged, and spent itself, yet, afterwards, among the sunshine was the strange lurking and wandering of the electric currents, moving invisible, with strange menace, between the atoms of the air. She knew. Oh, she knew!

And her love for her ranch turned sometimes into a certain repulsion. The underlying rat-dirt, the everlasting bristling tussle of the wild life, with the tangle and the bones strewing: Bones of horses struck by lightning, bones of dead cattle, skulls of goats with little horns: bleached, unburied bones. Then the cruel electricity of the mountains. And then, most mysterious but worst of all, the animosity of the spirit of place: the crude, half-created spirit of place, like some serpent-bird for ever attacking man, in a hatred of man's onward struggle towards further creation.

The seething cauldron of lower life, seething on the very tissue of the higher life, seething the soul away, seething at the marrow. The vast and unrelenting will of the swarming lower life, working forever against man's attempt at a higher life, a further created being.

At last, after many years, the little woman admitted to herself that she was glad to go down from the ranch, when November came with snows. She was glad to come to a more human home, her house in the village. And as winter passed by and spring came again, she knew she did not want to go up to the ranch again. It had broken something in her. It had hurt her terribly. It had maimed her for ever in her hope, her belief in paradise on earth. Now she hid from herself her own corpse, the corpse of her New England belief in a world ultimately all for love. The belief, and herself with it, was a corpse. The gods of those inner mountains were grim and invidious and relentless, huger than man, and lower than man. Yet man could never master them.

The little woman in her flower-garden away below, by the stream-irrigated village, hid away from the thought of it all. She would not go to the ranch any more.

The Mexicans stayed in charge, looking after the goats. But the place didn't pay. It didn't pay, not quite. It had paid. It might pay. But the effort, the effort! And as the marrow is eaten out of a man's bones and the soul out of his belly, contending with the strange rapacity of savage life, the lower stage of creation, he cannot make the effort any more.

Then also, the war came, making many men give up their enterprises at civilisation.

Every new stroke of civilisation has cost the lives of countless brave men, who have fallen defeated by the 'dragon', in their efforts to win the apples of the Hesperides, or the fleece of gold. Fallen in their efforts to overcome the old, half-sordid savagery of the lower stages of creation, and win to the next stage.

For all savagery is half sordid. And man is only himself when he is fighting on and on, to overcome the sordidness. And every civilisation, when it loses its inward vision and its cleaner energy, falls into a new sort of sordidness, more vast and more stupendous than the old savage sort. An Augean stable of metallic filth.

And all the time, man has to rouse himself afresh to cleanse the new accumulations of refuse. To win from the crude, wild nature the victory and the power to make another start, and to cleanse behind him the century-deep deposits of layer upon layer of refuse: even of tin cans.

The ranch dwindled. The flock of goats declined. The water ceased to flow. And at length the trader gave it up.

He rented the place to a Mexican, who lived on the handful of beans he raised, and who was being slowly driven out by the vermin.

And now arrived Lou, new blood to the attack. She went back to Santa Fe, saw the trader and a lawyer, and bought the ranch for twelve hundred dollars. She was so pleased with herself.

She sent upstairs to tell her mother.

"Mother, I've bought a ranch."

"It is just as well, for I can't stand the noise of automobiles outside here another week."

"It is quiet on my ranch, mother: the stillness simply speaks."

"I had rather it held its tongue. I am simply drugged with all the bad novels I have read. I feel as if the sky was a big cracked bell and a million clappers were hammering human speech out of it."

"Aren't you interested in my ranch, mother?"

"I hope I may be, by and by."

Mrs. Witt actually got up the next morning and accompanied her daughter in the hired motor-car, driven by Phoenix, to the ranch: which was called Las Chivas. She sat like a pillar of salt, her face looking what the Indians call a False Face, meaning a mask. She seemed to have crystallised into r neutrality. She watched the desert with its tufts of yellow greasewood go lurching past: she saw the fallen apples on the ground in the orchards near the adobe cottages: she looked down into the deep arroyo, and at the stream they forded hi, the car, and at the mountains blocking up the sky ahead, all with indifference. High on the mountains was snow: lower, blue-grey livid rock: and below the livid rock the aspens were expiring their daffodil yellow, this year, and the oak scrub was dark and reddish, like gore. She saw it all with a sort of stony indifference.

"Don't you think it's lovely?" said Lou.

"I can *see* it is lovely," replied her mother.

The Michaelmas daisies in the clearing as they drove up to the ranch were sharp-rayed with purple, like a coming night. Mrs. Witt eyed the two log cabins, one of which was dilapidated and practically abandoned. She looked at the rather rickety corral, whose long planks had silvered and warped in the fierce sun. On one of the roof-planks a pack-rat was sitting erect like an old Indian keeping watch on a pueblo roof. He showed his white belly, and folded his hands and lifted his big ears, for all the world like an old immobile Indian.

"Isn't it for all the world as if he were the real boss of the place, Louise?" she said cynically.

And turning to the Mexican, who was a rag of a man but a pleasant, courteous fellow, she asked him why he didn't shoot the rat.

"Not worth a shell!" said the Mexican, with a faint, hopeless smile.

Mrs. Witt paced round and saw everything: it did not take long. She gazed in silence at the water of the spring, trickling out of an iron pipe into a barrel, under the cotton-wood tree in an arroyo.

"Well, Louise," she said. "I am glad you feel competent to cope with so much hopelessness and so many rats."

"But, mother, you must admit it is beautiful."

"Yes, I suppose it is. But to use one of your Henry's phrases, beauty is a cold egg, as far as I am concerned."

"Rico never would have said that beauty was a cold egg to him."

"No, he wouldn't. He sits on it like a broody old hen on a china imitation.--Are you going to bring him here?"

"*Bring* him I--No. But he can come if he likes," stammered Lou.

"Oh--*h*! won't it be beau--ti--ful!" cried Mrs. Witt, rolling her head and lifting her shoulders in savage imitation of her son-in-law.

"Perhaps he won't come, mother," said Lou, hurt.

"He will most certainly come, Louise, to see what's doing: unless you tell him you don't want him."

"Anyhow, I needn't think about it till spring," said Lou, anxiously pushing the matter aside.

Mrs. Witt climbed the steep slope above the cabins to the mouth of the little canyon. There she sat on a fallen tree and surveyed the world beyond: a world not of men. She could not fail to be roused.

"What is your idea in coming here, daughter?" she asked. "I love it here, mother."

"But what do you expect to achieve by it?"

"I was rather hoping, mother, to escape achievement. I'll tell you--and you mustn't get cross if it sounds silly. As far as people go, my heart is quite broken. And far as people go, I don't want any more. I can't stand any more. What heart I ever had for it--for life with people--is quite broken. I want to be alone, mother: with you here, and Phoenix perhaps to look after horses and drive a car. But I want to be by myself, really."

"With Phoenix in the background! Are you sure he won't be coming into the foreground before long?"

"No, mother, no more of that. If I've got to say it, Phoenix is a servant: he's really placed, as far as I can see. Always the same, playing about in the old back yard. I can't take those men seriously. I can't fool round with them, or fool myself about them. I can't and I won't fool myself any more, mother, especially about men. They don't count. So why should you want them to pay me out?"

For the moment, this silenced Mrs. Witt. Then she said:

"Why, *I* don't want it. Why should I? But after all, you've got to live. You've never *lived* yet: not in my opinion."

"Neither, mother, in my opinion, have you," said Lou dryly.

And this silenced Mrs. Witt altogether. She had to be silent, or angrily on the defensive. And the latter she wouldn't be. She couldn't really, in honesty.

"What do you call life?" Lou continued. "Wriggling half naked at a public show and going off in a taxi to sleep with some half-drunken fool who thinks he's a man because--Oh, mother, I don't even want to think of it. I know you have a lurking idea that *that is life*. Let it be so then. But leave me, out. Men in that aspect simply nauseate me: so grovelling and ratty. Life in that aspect simply drains all my life away. I tell you, for all that sort of thing, I'm broken, absolutely broken: if I wasn't broken to start with."

"Well, Louise," said Mrs. Witt after a pause, "I'm convinced that ever since men and women were men and women, people who took things seriously, and had time for it, got their hearts broken. Haven't I had mine broken! It's as sure as having your virginity broken: and it amounts to about as much. It's a beginning rather than an end."

"So it is, mother. It's the beginning of something else, and the end of something that's done with. I *know*, and there's no altering it, that I've got to live differently. It sounds silly, but I don't know how else to put it. I've got to live for something that matters, way, way down in me. And I think sex would matter, to my very soul, if it was really sacred. But cheap sex kills me."

"You have had a fancy for rather cheap men, perhaps."

"Perhaps I have. Perhaps I should always be a fool, where people are concerned. Now I want to leave off that kind of foolery. There's something else, mother, that I want to give myself to. I know it. I know it absolutely. Why should I let myself be shouted down any more?"

Mrs. Witt sat staring at the distance, her face a cynical mask.

"What is the something bigger? And *pray*, what is it bigger than?" she asked, in that tone of honeyed suavity which was her deadliest poison. "I want to learn. I am out to know. I'm terribly intrigued by it. Something bigger! Girls in my generation occasionally entered convents for *something bigger*. I always wondered if they found it. They seemed to me inclined in the imbecile direction, but perhaps that was because I was *something less--*"

There was a definite pause between the mother and daughter, a silence that was a pure breach. Then Lou said:

"You know quite well I'm not conventy, mother, whatever else I am--even a bit of an imbecile. But that kind of religion seems to me the other half of men. Instead of running after them you run away from them, and get the thrill that way. I don't hate men *because* they're men, as nuns do. I dislike them because they're not men enough: babies, and playboys, and poor things showing off all the time, even to themselves.

"I don't say I'm any better. I only wish, with all my soul, that some men were bigger and stronger and *deeper* than I am..."

"How do you know they're not?--" asked Mrs. Witt.

"How *do* I know?--" said Lou mockingly.

And the pause that was a breach resumed itself. Mrs. Witt was teasing with a little stick the bewildered black ants among the fir-needles.

"And no doubt you are right about men," she said at length. "But at your age, the only sensible thing is to try and keep up the illusion. After all, as you say, you may be no better."

"I may be no better. But keeping up the illusion means fooling myself. And I won't do it. When I see a man who is even a bit attractive to me--even as much as Phoenix--I say to myself: 'Would you care for him afterwards? Does he really mean anything to you, except just a sensation?'--And I know he doesn't. No, mother, of this I am convinced: either my taking a man shall have a meaning and a mystery that penetrates my very soul, or I will keep to myself.--And what I know is, that the time has come for me to keep to myself. No more messing about."

"Very well, daughter. You will probably spend your life keeping to yourself."

"Do you think I mind! There's something else for me, mother. There's something else even that loves me and wants me. I can't tell you what it is. It's a spirit. And it's here, on this ranch. It's here, in this landscape. It's something more real to me than men are, and it soothes me, and it holds me up. I don't know what it is, definitely. It's something wild, that will hurt me sometimes and will wear me down sometimes. I know it. But it's something big, bigger than men, bigger than people, bigger than religion. It's something to do with wild America. And it's something to do with me. It's a mission, if you like. I am imbecile enough for that!--But it's my mission to keep myself for the spirit that is wild, and has waited so long here: even waited for such as me. Now I've come! Now I'm here. Now I am where I want to be: with the spirit that wants me.--And that's how it is. And neither Rico nor Phoenix nor anybody else really matters to me. They are in the world's backyard. And I am here, right deep in America, where there's a wild spirit wants me, a wild spirit more than men. And it doesn't want to save me either. It needs me. It craves for me. And to it, my sex is deep and sacred, deeper than I am, with a deep nature aware deep down of my sex. It saves me from cheapness, mother. And even you could never do that for me."

Mrs. Witt rose to her feet and stood looking far, far away at the turquoise ridge of mountains half sunk under the horizon.

"How much did you say you paid for Las Chivas?" she asked

"Twelve hundred dollars," said Lou, surprised.

"Then I call it cheap, considering all there is to it: even the name."

THE END

Lector House believes that a society develops through a two-fold approach of continuous learning and adaptation, which is derived from the study of classic literary works spread across the historic timeline of literature records. Therefore, we aim at reviving, repairing and redeveloping all those inaccessible or damaged but historically as well as culturally important literature across subjects so that the future generations may have an opportunity to study and learn from past works to embark upon a journey of creating a better future.

This book is a result of an effort made by Lector House towards making a contribution to the preservation and repair of original ancient works which might hold historical significance to the approach of continuous learning across subjects.

HAPPY READING & LEARNING!

LECTOR HOUSE LLP
E-MAIL: lectorpublishing@gmail.com

www.ingramcontent.com/pod-product-compliance
Lightning Source LLC
LaVergne TN
LVHW090541060426
835515LV00040B/1886